Kiss the Girls and Make Them Cry

Kiss the Girls and Make Them Cry

Brittani Williams

www.urbanbooks.net

Urban Books, LLC
300 Farmingdale Road, NY-Route 109
Farmingdale, NY 11735

Kiss the Girls and Make Them Cry

ISBN 13: 978-1-62286-634-2
ISBN 10: 1-62286-634-7

First Trade Paperback Printing March 2018
Printed in the United States of America

10 9 8 7 6 5 4 3 2 1

Distributed by Kensington Publishing Corp.
Submit orders to:
Customer Service
400 Hahn Road
Westminster, MD 21157-4627
Phone: 1-800-733-3000
Fax: 1-800-659-2436

Kiss the Girls and Make Them Cry

by

Brittani Williams

Prologue

One Night Changes Everything

"I'll meet you at home, baby. I'm going to finish up a few things and make sure all of the ladies are out of here safely," Richard said to Nancy as she headed toward the exit of the nightclub.

"That better be all that you're doing," she said, rolling her eyes.

"What's that for?" he asked, walking closer to her.

"Don't act like you don't know what I'm talking about. You know I have eyes everywhere, and you most certainly are not an angel, Richard." She twisted her lips.

Her distrust was birthed from a combination of infidelity and a lack of self-confidence. It isn't unusual for a woman to question her own abilities after being cheated on. Their courtship had always been a challenge. Though she wanted to trust her husband, it was his behavior and periods of disrespect that always threatened their stability.

"Babe, I'm extremely tired, and I really don't feel like arguing with you every night that I'm here closing up. I'm taking care of business; mind you, it's a business that allows you to wear those expensive shoes you have on your feet. Instead of allowing me to do what I need to do for our family, you chose to argue with me in the middle of the club," he raised his voice.

"I'm not arguing with you, Richard. I made one simple statement. Don't you dare try to come at me as if *I'm* the problem in this marriage. If you could learn how to keep your dick in your pants, we wouldn't have anything to argue about, now, would we?" she raised her voice as well.

"Are we *really* going to do this right now?" he said, shaking his head.

"You know what? I'm done with this conversation. I'll see you when you get home." She rolled her eyes again before disappearing from his view.

Richard had been known to sleep with dancers at the club that he owned. Even though his wife was beautiful, it was extremely hard to resist the vixens that worked for him. His eyes constantly wandered, but somehow, he'd always been able to convince Nancy to forgive him. Each time he'd been caught, he'd buy her something expensive and hit her with those puppy dog eyes, winning her over. Though they fought a lot, it never changed the amount of love they had for each other. From the outside looking in, they were the perfect couple. Almost like the modern-day Cosbys, with a twist. They were extremely successful, but being the owners of an exotic dancing club couldn't compare to that of the prestigious Huxtable couple. They were hood successful, but he wasn't highly educated like Cliff, and she wasn't the successful attorney like Clair. Though their achievements came from years of hard work, none of it came legally.

As far as the appearance of their relationship, unless you were one of their employees, you'd assume that they were the model couple, what most would call couple goals. The truth was, they were more of a business partnership than anything else. They knew how to put on big smiles and social functions, and convince the world that they were happy. But soon, the attraction was gone, and there wasn't any amount of money that could buy that back. Nancy just learned how to play nice and be the trophy wife that she needed to be.

It was a normal evening, the club had brought in a ton money, and it was time to check the books, put the proceeds in the safe, walk through with security, and make sure that all of the women had been escorted out to their vehicles. Then he headed up to his office and nodded at the guard who stood outside of his office at all times. He closed the door behind him and took a seat at his desk. As usual, he went over the books and put away the money before locking up the safe. Then he sat down at the desk again for a moment and looked down at his phone. There was a message from one of the dancers at the club. He replied to tell her to come up to the office so they could talk.

A few moments later, there was a knock at the door. The security guard peeped in and let Richard know that the dancer Lovely D was here for him. He nodded, confirming that it was OK to let her in.

"Aye, do me a favor. Don't let anyone in for a little bit. I need to have a talk with her in private, all right?" Richard said as Lovely D walked into the room still dressed in her performance attire.

"No problem," the guard said before closing the door behind him.

"So what can I do for you?" Richard asked while licking his lips.

Lovely D stood there stacked like a purebred stallion. She had a perfect set of double-D breasts, a small waist, a phat ass, and phat pussy to match. It was nearly impossible for any man to avoid salivating when she walked into a room. She was just one on a long list of dancers that would occasionally meet Richard in his office after hours to "talk."

"You already know what you can do for me," she said, walking over toward his chair.

"It's better when I can hear it. Let me know what the problem is, and I'll try my best to solve it," he said, feeling his dick begin to swell in his pants.

Lovely D leaned back and gently slid onto his desk. She immediately pulled her thong to the side and took one finger to massage her throbbing clitoris. After she was satisfied with the amount of juices on her finger, she put her finger inside of his mouth and allowed him to lick it off before speaking. "You can come eat this pussy. That's what I need you to do for me," she said while biting her bottom lip.

"Damn," he said aloud while briefly rubbing his dick through his jeans. He moved in close while she held her thong with one hand and spread her pussy lips apart with the other. His warm tongue making contact with her clit immediately caused her to release a moan. She was nearly about to come on contact, but she was able to relax enough to enjoy it. Richard was amazing at giving head, almost like a professional. It didn't hurt that he had the long bank account to go along with the long dick inside his pants. For an older man, he knew how to handle the young women. It didn't matter how good they were with aerobics, he held his own every time. She leaned back to give him more room to work. He slurped and licked her pussy in circles for the next ten minutes, bringing on one orgasm after another. Her body was trembling and releasing all inside of his mouth.

"I need you to fuck me, daddy," she said in a sexy whisper.

Without hesitation, he stood up, unbuttoned his pants, dropped them to the floor, and pulled out his thick piece of meat.

"I need you to suck this dick first. Suck it real good for daddy," he said while guiding her off of the desk and down on her knees.

She wrapped her lips around his dick and began working her magic. One thing was for certain about the girls that worked inside of his club, they knew how to give some bomb-ass head. With a little movement, he thrust his hips, forcing his dick deeper into her throat. Without any gagging at all, she continued to suck his dick and massage his balls at the same time. He was in heaven on earth at that moment. He didn't want to waste any more time, so he pulled her up and bent her over the desk. He rubbed the head of his dick up against her wetness before pushing it all inside. His balls slapped up against her ass every time he went deep inside. He grabbed hold of her long ponytail and used it to get deeper inside. She was moaning and screaming his name.

Outside of the room, the security guard was laughing as he heard the entire sex scene through the door. He was used to these late-night "meetings." There were always pretty women around Richard, so he knew that in the event Nancy returned, he could notify Richard before he was caught with his pants down. After another twenty minutes, Lovely D was back on her knees with her mouth opened wide, ready to swallow all of his come.

"Damn, girl," Richard said as she was sucking him bone dry. He slapped his dick up against her lips a few times before pulling his pants back up and sitting down. As she fixed her costume, he reached into his drawer and pulled out a stack of hundreds. He placed it in her hands as she smiled and headed toward the door.

The security guard couldn't help but laugh as Lovely D swished down the hall with remnants of come on her face.

"You a wild boy, Richard," he said, as he laughed and closed the door again.

Richard looked down at his phone and noticed that Nancy had called him several times. He'd been so deep in Lovely D that he didn't feel the phone vibrating.

He called her back a few times, but she didn't answer. Then he gathered up the remainder of his things, turned off the lights to his office, and walked toward the door. Before he could shut the door behind him, he and the guard backed up as four masked men ran up the stairs. The guard drew his gun and attempted to push Richard inside of the office to safety. Neither of them were a match for the men who came armed and ready to kill. The guard's gun flew in the air as he fell backward into the door. The door was forced open by the weight of the guard as he fell to the floor. Richard hadn't gotten a chance to lock the door behind him. A scuffle ensued as two of the intruders held the guard on the floor. One of the other men immediately grabbed Richard while the other pointed his gun in his face.

"I'll give you whatever you want. You can have everything in the safe, just please don't kill me," Richard pleaded.

"Open the fucking safe," one of the men yelled.

Richard did as he was told and opened the safe. In his mind, he thought that if he cooperated with the men, his life would be spared. This wasn't the first time he'd been robbed. There were always people plotting on business owners like him. They could estimate the amount of money the club brought in because of the long lines and packed parking lots. He assumed that this time would be just like any other time. He'd truly underestimated the criminals that stood behind him with multiple guns pointed in his direction. His gift of gab wouldn't cut it this time.

Richard stood beside the men as they gathered up all of the money and valuables from the safe. Suddenly, his phone began to ring, and for a brief second, everyone paused. By the second ring, they had resumed packing up their bags with goods. The phone continued to ring, and the men ignored it as well as Richard. Richard saw their moment of distraction as his chance to grab his phone which had landed on the floor a few feet away when he was pushed inside of the office. He turned to make a dash for his phone, causing everyone in the room to stop what they were doing and focus on him.

"Just kill this nigga," one of the men holding the guard at gunpoint said.

The masked men immediately began firing and filling Richard's body with bullets.

On the other end of the phone, Nancy tried to return Richard's call, unaware of the carnage that was currently laid out over the floor. She called him over and over, leaving him multiple angry voice messages. The majority of them were accusing him of being somewhere with a woman. Though less than an hour earlier that had been the case, while she continued to yell into the phone, she had no idea that this would be the last time she'd ever hear his voice again. It's amazing how one night can truly change your life.

Chapter One

Once again it was Monday night, and beautiful women, both young and old, were packed inside Philly's number one male exotic strip club, Club Chances. There wasn't a club in Philly that could bring the city out like this. Women from New Jersey, Delaware, Baltimore, and some as far away as New York City, would all show up at Club Chances, dressed in the latest designer fashions, smelling and looking their very best. The women would come in trying to show one another that they could get the most attention. There were a few women that wouldn't be happy unless all of the other attendees weren't looking on full of envy.

Club Chances was large and spacious with a long main stage, several smaller stages off to the side, two floors, and small round tables that were situated all throughout the club. Upstairs on the second floor were private rooms and the elegant VIP section, for all the *special* customers. These customers were the women willing to spend their entire paycheck on a little bit of time from some of the clubs most sought out dancers. Of course, there were Champagne Rooms for that *extra special* attention.

Every Monday and Wednesday night, the only nights the top dancers performed their signature shows, the club would be filled with hundreds of lonely, horny, and desperate women who patiently waited in the long line outside that curved around the building. There were two admission prices to enter. The lowest price was thirty dollars which only included entrance into the club without any extra amenities. For this price, you wouldn't have access to the main stage. You'd be limited to the small stages with the hopes of catching a glimpse of the main attraction.

Then there was the second price of $100, which would allow your access to the entire club. You'd have a seat at the main stage and be able to reach out and touch those who performed there. You'd also have access to bottle service and the buffet of finger foods provided by a local soul food restaurant called Tasties. The 300 lucky women that made it inside had no problem with paying the cover charge or throwing out their rent money at the muscular dancers who performed there. For the unfortunate women that didn't make it inside the club, they would all just show up for the next show, which could be the next week if it was Wednesday, and try their luck again. Filling the club was never a problem, and if it wasn't for the fire safety codes, it would be filled up even more.

Nancy Robinson stood on the upstairs balcony watching as all the women walked through the entrance. She had a big smile on her face because every time a woman walked through those doors, there was more money going into her already fully loaded bank account. Nancy was the forty-year-old owner of Club Chances. After her husband, Richard, had been killed in a robbery, she had taken complete control of the club. The first thing that Nancy had done was change the club format from female exotic dancers to exotic male strippers. She believed that if she opened the doors to women, she would make more of a profit. Sure, the club was successful when it was a female club, but men weren't willing to spend as much money as the women were, and women always bought a lot more drama along with it. She always said it was one of the best decisions she'd ever made because the money started pouring in by the truckloads. She was able to make even more money than her late husband did, and she was also able to avoid the fights and other bull that he dealt with in the past. She didn't have time for that nonsense. She was all about her business, and the men were most definitely eye candy, but she wasn't about to allow a hard dick to screw up her business, or even more, her life. One of the biggest mistakes that her husband made was getting involved with too many dancers, and allowing that weakness to get him killed.

Nancy was a dark-skinned woman with average looks. She stood at five foot four and 130 pounds. For her age, her body was still in tiptop condition. Twice a week she'd give her body everything it needed to maintain. She never missed her appointment with her personal trainer at the downtown Bally's gym. Nancy was as sharp as they came when she handled her business at the club. She was a firm believer in being healthy on the inside as well as the outside. She made sure that she always ate right, and working out only made her feel her best. Running a business like hers required a lot of energy; energy that she was well equipped with due to her healthy lifestyle.

Just as strict as she was with maintaining her body, she was with her business. At least three times a week she would thoroughly go through all of the books. If she found that the numbers didn't match up, she would come in and go completely off. Over the years, she'd learned to be a little more professional with her approach, but she still wanted people to fear her wrath; otherwise, she'd be run over. There was no way that she would be known as a pushover, and being a woman who employed 95 percent men, being soft wasn't an option. Everyone knew not to play with Nancy, especially when money was involved. Her anger could go from zero to 100 real quick, and it was best to stay out of her way. This was the way that she liked it, and the only way that she believed that she would maintain order. Some would say that she was a real bitch, and that was OK with Nancy. You'd never hear her try to claim that she was an angel instead. Most likely, she'd claim that she was not only a bitch, but the *baddest* bitch you'd ever meet.

Now, when it came to friends and socializing, she was a woman with few friends, mainly because she had trust issues. Over the span of her lifetime, she'd been betrayed by many women who called themselves her friend. One in particular was her one time best friend Gloria. The two had done everything together, and for many years, you wouldn't see one without the other. As close as their friendship was, she would never have guessed that Gloria was sleeping with her husband. Not only had they been sleeping together, but they'd carried on a five-year affair and had a child together. When Nancy found out, she was devastated. She'd spent countless hours with their child and had even been made the godmother—only later to find out their secret.

Nancy was never privy to the identity of the child's father. Gloria told her that she wanted him to remain nameless for the protection of their child. Being the type of friend that Nancy was, she respected her choice and didn't ask again. Their children played together and began grooming their own close bond. Learning of their betrayal was almost enough to send Nancy straight to the psychiatric ward. There wasn't anything that anyone could tell you, nor anything that you could read inside of a book that could prepare you for this kind of heartbreak. The news couldn't have come at a worse time either.

Gloria had been planning a huge birthday celebration for her daughter. At this time, Nancy's daughter was just ten years old. Gloria had shared every detail with Nancy, from the dress that her daughter would wear down to the table decorations and party favors. Nancy was excellent with décor, so it was natural for people to ask her opinion when it came to decorating an event from top to bottom. Not that Nancy wanted to be all in her pockets, but she knew that Gloria didn't have a whole lot of money so as she watched her spend thousands on this birthday party, she couldn't help but wonder where the funds were coming from.

"Girl, I hate to seem nosy, but I'm just wondering where the hell you got all this money from. You're always so frugal, I would never imagine you dropping $10,000 on your child's fifth birthday party," Nancy laughed.

"Girl, it's from her daddy. He was nice enough to give me his American Express Card to take care of everything. I would never spend this amount of my own money," she said, as she piled things onto the party store register belt.

"Oh, so he's helping now? Since when?" Nancy asked, surprised by the information.

"He never stopped helping with her. I never said that. I just said I didn't want to tell you who he was. He's always done for her," she snapped.

This was news to Nancy because she'd never heard anything about him assisting with anything financially. Though she never understood why Gloria wouldn't reveal his identity, she was OK with not knowing. She believed that they were as close as friends could be, but it wasn't until this moment that she realized that may not have been the case. She'd shared everything in her life with Gloria, and never knew much about her, come to think of it. Sure, some people were just that private, and she tried to chalk it up as that, but there were just some things that she didn't believe should be hidden from your "best friend."

"Well, I won't pry anymore," Nancy said.

The two continued shopping, but there was certainly an awkwardness in the air after their outing. They didn't even talk as much in the next week leading up to the birthday bash. Something about that shopping trip was nagging Nancy. Not to mention the fact that her husband, who barely ever attended any of their own daughter's parties, was planning on attending. It was all strange; something just wasn't right. You know how they tell you to trust your gut? Well, she decided to check her husband's credit card activity. Anyone else would've thought that Nancy was just overthinking, that she was just searching for something to be wrong. She'd prepared herself for the worst because of the way Gloria kept so many secrets, the way that she somehow was able to spend so much on a party, the way that a father would be willing to drop ten thousand on a party but not be in his child's life. Then, the way that Gloria made sure to cover the name on the credit card as she passed it to the cashier in the store. It wouldn't have meant anything any other time, but she did notice the first two letters on the name which were "Ri." Had she been overreacting, she'd be relieved, but lo and behold, when she pulled those records, there was all the evidence she needed to confirm every suspicion that she'd ever had.

There, staring her right in the face, were all of the charges from the party store. The dates and times matching up with the time that they were there. Her hands were shaking she was so furious. Was this enough to confront them both? She was sure at this moment that they'd committed the ultimate deceit. Though Richard had cheated on her many times before, this time was something altogether different. She looked at Gloria as more than a best friend, more like a sister. How could someone whom she would jump in front of a bullet for betray her this way?

So many thoughts were running through her head at that moment. She was sure that she'd commit murder and go to prison for the rest of her life if she didn't calm herself down. In her mind, it would be worth it, but then again, she had a daughter to be there for, and what good would her daughter be with a dead father and a mother behind bars? So she pulled it together. She figured that the best way to make them feel the pain that she felt would be to publicly embarrass them. To show them that they'd messed with the wrong bitch. She wasn't going to approach her husband at home. Nope, that was too easy. She was going to play nice and show up at that party and show her ass. This was the first time that she'd been so angry about one of his affairs that she would be willing to act like a fool in public. She didn't care what people would think. Everything that Gloria had coming to her would be well deserved.

The place was decorated from top to bottom in pink, white, and silver. There was glitter and confetti all over the place. Gloria made sure that this would be a party to remember. The place looked like something out of a magazine, or better yet, like something that you'd see on TV. There was a huge ice sculpture at the front of the room near the buffet that was shaped like a unicorn. Besides the color pink, there was only one thing that fascinated her daughter just as much, and that was the mystery surrounding the unicorn. Everywhere you looked there was glitter. Gloria just stood and giggled as her little girl walked around looking at everything thing and shouting, "This is the best birthday ever!"

Gloria stood there proud and feeling accomplished, oblivious to the destruction that would be coming her way shortly. She walked over to her daughter and gave her a big hug.

Not long after that, Richard arrived with gifts in hand. All of her life, the child had been told that this was her uncle. She had a lot of love for him and the way that he spoiled her. He arrived with a huge gift bag that he handed to her to put on her gift table. As he and Gloria embraced, he whispered something in her ear, and she laughed. A few moments later, Nancy entered the party. You could tell that she didn't come to party. She had the look of death spewed all across her face. Her daughter, whom she'd left in the car, would be spared from the scene that was about to play out.

"Well, let me in on the joke," Nancy said with her face twisted.

Both of them turned to look at her, not sure what she was speaking about.

"What joke?" Gloria asked.

"Whatever the joke was that has you laughing. Whatever he whispered in your fucking ear!" she yelled.

"Nancy, what's wrong with you? Why are you yelling?" Richard asked, noticing a huge shift in her attitude than when he exited the car a few moments earlier.

"You know, you too much really thinking I'm fucking stupid, huh? Did you really think that I would never figure this out?"

Both of them stood there visibly uncomfortable. Guests were starting to notice that something was amiss.

"Nancy, I'm not sure what you are implying, but this is not the time—or the place—to have this conversation, if there is one to be had. I don't know what you think you saw, but there was nothing inappropriate said just now," Gloria said, trying to calm Nancy down and somehow diffuse the situation that was brewing.

"Bitch, I trusted you. You've been my friend for twenty fucking years, and this is the way that you repay me?"

"Now, that's enough, Nancy," Richard yelled, grabbing her by the arm.

Snatching her arm away from him she yelled, "Get your fucking filthy hands off of me! You are nothing but a cheating bastard and a liar. You two disgust me!"

"Could we take this outside, Nancy, please? This is ruining my daughter's birthday party," Gloria pleaded.

"The party that my husband paid for with our fucking credit card? Huh? Didn't think I would notice you trying to cover his name, bitch, did you? Well, guess what? I have the credit card statement. Since I'm his wife, I have access to that," she yelled as she pulled the papers from her back pocket and threw them in Gloria's face.

The papers fell to the floor. By this point, everyone in attendance had their eyes glued on the threesome, trying to figure out what was going on. They all knew Nancy and had never witnessed the two women have any type of disagreement. If they'd had one, it was done behind closed doors, so this was a shock to everyone.

"Nancy, please, let's go outside," Richard said.

"I'm not going any-fucking-where until I'm done, and since I have everyone's attention, I might as well speak to all of you too. This bitch here—that I thought was my friend—has been fucking my husband!"

You immediately heard loud gasps coming from all over the room. Everyone was shocked, looking for the main event because it was sure to come.

"Not only has she been fucking my husband, but this bitch had a child by him and had the audacity to make me the godmother!"

More gasps filled the air. Both Richard and Gloria stood there in stunned silence.

"Cat got your tongues?" Nancy yelled.

"I can't believe that you would come to a child's birthday party to do this, Nancy. You really could've spoken to me in private," Gloria said.

"You don't believe me? Really, bitch? You have some fucking nerve to stand here and act all high and mighty after what you've done to me."

"Nancy, can we please go home and deal with this privately—please?" Richard asked.

"I'm not leaving until I'm done."

"What else is there for you to do, Nance?" Gloria asked.

"This," Nancy said as she began pounding Gloria with closed fists. Gloria fell to the floor unable to keep her balance and defend herself. She screamed as Nancy landed punch after punch all across her face. You could hear the children screaming in the background. Even as Richard and a few other guests tried to pull Nancy off of Gloria, her anger and adrenaline fueled strength that couldn't be broken. Though the fight would only last a few minutes, it was enough time to leave Gloria with a busted nose, lip, and a black eye which was quickly swelling and discoloring. When they finally freed Gloria from her grasp, she screamed obscenities the entire time she walked toward the door. Richard was furious, but Nancy didn't care one bit. She'd done what she'd come to do—fuck shit up.

That day changed their relationship. It was at that moment when she stopped being physically attracted to Richard. It was that moment when she knew that she'd never want to be touched by him sexually again. There was a point when she contemplated getting a divorce, but she wasn't about to let him go play house with Gloria. She never spoke to Gloria again after that day. She never even ran into her in passing. It was about a month later when she learned that Gloria had packed up and moved to New Jersey. After this, Nancy would never allow a woman to be this close to her again. Gloria had tarnished any thought of real friendship that Nancy had.

Due to her lack of trust in women, she would sit back and watch your behavior until she was able to figure you out. If she felt that you couldn't be trusted, she would cut you off without any hesitation. Most of the time, she stayed to herself, and that was just the way she liked it. When Nancy wasn't overlooking the daily operations of the club, which was rare, her beautiful, tall, twenty-two-year-old daughter India took over the responsibilities.

Now, India was the total opposite of her mother. Everyone genuinely liked India. It was extremely rare to find someone that had anything negative to say about her. She was just as beautiful, if not more beautiful, on the inside as she was on the outside. She had a warm, pleasant spirit that attracted almost everyone who came near her. Not to mention the fact that she had a smile so beautiful that it could make the hardest man melt right into the palm of her hand. India had a honey-brown complexion. She stood five foot nine, weighed 135 pounds, with a slim, hourglass figure. Most of the dancers who worked at the club had tried numerous times to get with India, but just like most of the women who poured into Club Chances every Monday and Wednesday night, India had her eyes focused on only one. The man that had the attention of all of the ladies was Ricky, better known as "Mr. Orgasm." Ricky was the sole reason that Club Chances was sold out every Monday and Wednesday. There was no doubt that women from all over the tristate area would drive to Philly and wait outside in those ridiculously long lines. They all wanted to get a look, taste, touch, or a sample of the famous exotic dancer they called "Mr. Orgasm."

Ricky, along with nineteen other male strippers, would show up twice a week and give all of their creaming, horny fans the show of their lives. Still, none of the other male exotic dancers were as popular as the tall, dark, and handsome "Mr. Orgasm." Ricky stood at six foot five and 195 pounds of solid muscle. He had a smooth, dark brown complexion, which covered his well-sculpted physique. Whenever he smiled, his perfect white teeth would light up the entire room. Ricky kept his head shaved completely bald. The only hair that he had was on his face in a neatly trimmed and shaped-up goatee.

At twenty-seven years old, Ricky had the world in his hands: money, street fame, and a large supply of beautiful women that most men could only dream of. He could have any woman that he desired, but the true and only love of Ricky's young life was his six-year-old daughter, Asia. After Asia's mother died while giving birth to her, Ricky eagerly took over the responsibility of raising his beautiful newborn daughter alone. At the time, he was all prepared to make things work for his family. The day that his wife went in labor was fresh on his mind, as if it happened only yesterday.

It was a Saturday morning, and his plans to sleep in late were changed when he heard a loud scream from the other room. It startled him so much so that he almost fell to the floor jumping up to see what was happening. He looked around the room and immediately noticed that his wife wasn't in the bed next to him anymore. A second or two later, Toni yelled again from the bathroom.

"Ricky!" she screamed in a bloodcurdling tone.

Immediately, he ran toward the bathroom, slipping all across the hardwood floor in his socks. He'd never been so scared in his life. The way that she screamed confirmed that she was in extreme pain. He hadn't mentally prepared himself for the worst. Sure, people say that childbirth is the closest thing to death, but no one actually believes that the greatest day of one's life could also be the worst. Once he made it into the bathroom, Toni was sitting on the toilet in only her bra.

"What's happening? What's wrong?" he asked, quickly coming to her rescue.

"I think the baby is coming," she yelled as her entire body trembled. Tears were pouring from her eyes as she grabbed ahold of Ricky's hand, squeezing it as hard as she could.

"OK, what should I do? Do you want me to drive you to the hospital?" He couldn't even think straight.

Irritated, she yelled, "Get the phone and call 911!"

The last thing he wanted to do was upset her at a time like this, but he was truly clueless of what to do in a situation like this.

"OK, OK, I'll be right back," he said as he ran out of the bathroom and over to his phone that was resting on his bedside table.

His adrenaline was rushing, and his nerves were all over the place. He dropped the phone twice trying to dial 911. Once he got through, the operator asked him a series of questions. With his rattled nerves and her screams, he found it extremely difficult to follow the directions of the woman on the line. The few minutes that it took for the paramedics to arrive felt like an eternity.

He threw on a pair of sweatpants and a T-shirt before running out to his car to meet the ambulance at the hospital. Then he sped through the city toward Temple University Hospital. He prayed the entire time that he would arrive without causing an accident. Additionally, he prayed that both Toni and his baby girl would be OK when he arrived.

He made it to the hospital emergency room in record time. Running through the hall out of breath, he gave her name at the desk. They directed him to the labor and delivery unit. He was so impatient and afraid of missing the birth that he couldn't even wait on the elevator.

He literally ran up the stairs, skipping two or three steps at a time. Once on the floor, he was shown the way to the labor and delivery suite. He could hear Toni's cries through the hall. He ran into the room to be by her side. He'd never seen her in so much pain, and he wished that there were something that he could do to help her.

"You made it just in time. She's just about ready to push," the one African American nurse said.

"Oh my God, are you serious? Toni, did you hear that? Our baby girl is almost here!"

At that moment, his nervousness shifted to excitement. He'd waited for this day, and he couldn't wait to hold his baby girl in his arms and look her in the eyes. The nurses and doctor were moving at a fast pace to get in position. Once everyone was in place, it was time to push.

"OK, on the next contraction, I need you to bear down and push, OK? Hold it for ten seconds, take a breath, and do it again. Let's get this little girl out," the doctor said as the nurse showed Ricky how to hold her leg and assist.

On the first push, you could already see the head. Ricky was filled with many emotions. He'd never witnessed a woman giving birth. He was afraid of all of the things that he'd seen gone wrong in the movies. He loved Toni more than he'd loved anyone, and it would kill him to lose her. The way that he'd picture his daughter coming into the world wasn't filled with this kind of fear. There was a knot in his stomach, and at that moment, he didn't understand why. He said a silent prayer as he got in position and held Toni's leg for her to push. He was terrified of being a father but excited at the very same time. He wanted to be the perfect father. He didn't want to fail as his father had with him. He just wanted to be the best that he could be.

While he could visibly see how much pain that Toni was in, he could never imagine what it really felt like. She was stronger than he could ever be, and he would be forever grateful for having her in his life. There wasn't anything that could ever take the love and respect that he had for her away. She was giving him the greatest blessing that anyone could ever receive.

There were so many people in the room. So many people giving out directions that he wasn't sure what to do. Just when he thought he was holding her leg right, someone else would tell him to do it differently. There was a moment when he became frustrated, but he knew that showing it would only make things harder for Toni, so he held it together and did what he was told. She would push for what seemed like an eternity. Over an hour would pass, and she was still pushing and becoming more exhausted by the minute. For a moment, he was afraid that she wouldn't be able to do it.

"Baby, I know you're tired, but you're the strongest woman that I know. If anyone can do it, I know that you can do it. I'm right here with you, baby," he said. He didn't know what else to say at that moment, but he believed that encouragement was the way to go. Surely, that would give her the push that she needed to get the baby out.

She looked up at him with tears streaming down both sides of her face. "I can't do this, Ricky, I can't."

It almost made him cry seeing her in so much agony. He knew that he had to be strong and continue to encourage her.

"Toni, you're so close. She's almost here, baby. You've got this," he said.

After a few more rounds of pushing, the baby was out and immediately placed onto Toni's stomach. Through the oxygen mask, she smiled and cried tears of joy.

Looking at their baby girl was a blessing beyond what words could measure.

"You did it," Ricky said looking at his daughter and Toni.

It was one of the most beautiful things he'd experienced in his life. They took the baby over to the warmer as the doctor continued working to deliver Toni's afterbirth. Ricky looked at Asia in awe. He was mesmerized by how beautiful she was. He snapped pictures of her while she held on to his finger with her hands.

Suddenly, he heard a series of beeps and a lot of commotion. He looked over at Toni and realized that her body had gone limp, and her eyes were no longer open. It was almost as if he'd lost his hearing. All he could do was stand still looking at all of the people working to save her.

Both Ricky and the baby were taken out of the room. As he stood in the hall watching the barrage of medical professionals running into the room, he couldn't move. He hadn't even noticed that the nurse had taken the baby to the nursery. He could hear different types of medications being requested by the doctor. He had no idea what could've gone wrong so quickly. Almost in the blink of an eye, a happy moment turned to pure devastation. For what seemed like hours, he stood in the same spot saying silent prayers over and over in his head.

Finally, a nurse came out of the room and took him into the recovery waiting area. He didn't think that the reason was to give him the news privately. He wasn't ready, and it probably would be impossible to prepare for something like this. A minute or two later, the doctor that just delivered his baby informed him that Toni, the mother of his child, the woman that he would have a special love for the gift—was gone.

"This has to be a joke. Are you serious? You aren't serious? She's going to be OK, right? Come on, Doc, tell me that this isn't real." Tears fell from his eyes and began landing all over his shirt.

Despite their explanation of the cause, an amniotic fluid embolism, he couldn't wrap his mind around the fact that a very healthy woman had just died giving birth to his daughter. He couldn't process it, almost as if they had been speaking in another language. The way they explained it to him was that amniotic fluid from the uterus gets into the bloodstream and moves to your lungs. This can cause a heart attack or, ultimately, death. It happens so fast, and there often isn't enough time to save someone in this condition.

He couldn't even pull himself together when her parents arrived at the hospital. They expected to see their baby in their daughter's arms, only to hear the same devastating news that had been delivered to him only a few minutes earlier. It was unfathomable. He would forever have the thought of never seeing her again burned into his memory. At least he could find some comfort in the fact that even though it was only for a moment, Toni had been able to look into the eyes of the beautiful creation they were given.

Before she was removed from the room, Ricky made a promise to her that he would work as hard as he could to provide for their child. He refused to allow her to be without. He wanted her to have everything, as if she still had both parents, and never envy people who did. From that day forward, everything that he did was for her.

Despite his inexperience with children, Ricky did an exceptional job taking care of his little responsibility. Prior to her birth, he'd never even changed a diaper. He was terrified of being a single father, but he wasn't about to walk away from the greatest gift you could ever receive.

Before Asia, he never truly understood the meaning of unconditional love. For him, love always came with conditions, meaning if you hurt him in any way, his love for you would disappear. There wasn't anything that Asia could do to change his love for her, and he'd worked extremely hard to give her all of things that he didn't have as a child. Ricky spoiled Asia with all the love he could give her. He was also very picky with the women he brought around his young daughter. So most of the time, he and Asia would be alone. Watching TV, taking trips to the zoo, shopping, and all the other things that a young father and his six-year-old daughter could enjoy.

At the club, Ricky stood behind the large stage curtain, listening to the sounds of boisterous young and older women laughing and talking. He looked through the small hole in the curtain and saw the large crowd of women patiently waiting. The women who weren't sitting down at the tables were all gathered at the front edge of the stage, whistling, cheering, and clapping like adolescent young fans at a rap concert.

Ricky looked at the crowd and noticed all the regulars in attendance. Though there were some faces that he loved to see; there were a few that he didn't. Most of the women were perfect customers. He could shake his erect penis in their faces, take all of their money, and walk away without any additional expectations. Many of these women were there just for the thrill of watching him perform, so they weren't looking to be treated like anything other than a customer paying to watch a show. Then there were the other regulars that felt like he was their personal property. These were the women that would be ready to fight another chick if she got more attention from Ricky that she felt that she should. These were always the women who were the most quiet before he stepped onto the stage. They came with a sense of entitlement and expected him to ignore everyone else in the room. One of these women was sitting dead center, and her name was Octavia Bronx.

Octavia was a woman that most would love to spend time with. She was a seasoned woman unlike a lot of the women who frequented the club. You could tell that she'd been through a lot in her life by the way that she carried herself. She was always composed, but she would snap in a New York minute if someone got in her way. There was a mystery about her. She wasn't the thirsty type ready to throw her panties on the stage. She was just thirty-eight years old, but you'd think she was much older. Not because of her looks, because she could give a twenty-year-old a run for her money any day. Instead, it was her overall demeanor. It was almost as if she'd been here a lot longer than thirty-eight years.

Now, when speaking of her looks, she was a certified dime. She was fully equipped with all of the tools that women are willing to pay for. Hell, some of them are even willing to fly out of the country and risk their lives for a body like hers. Standing at about five foot six and weighing all of 135 pounds, she was curvy in all of the right places.

At times, Octavia could appear snobbish. Most of the women in the club wouldn't even sit near her. There was just an energy around her that was unexplainable. Either you wanted to know her, or you would go far in the other direction. When she walked in the club, all eyes would be on her. She walked with her head held high and wouldn't speak to anyone but those who she came in with. She was one of those that didn't travel in a big pack. Every week, she'd show up with the same two friends. They were always fashionably dressed. Designer gear from head to toe. Her nails were always perfectly manicured, and her hair was always laid to perfection.

Despite the fact that most of the women scowled as she walked by, she carried a huge smile and showed off her beautiful pearly whites. Now, one thing that you couldn't miss was the huge rock on her finger. She'd been married for over fifteen years. She would claim to the world that she was happy and that the only reason she attended the club weekly was for sheer entertainment. She was all about appearances, so she would drop dead before she would allow anyone to believe that her life was anything less than perfect. She claimed that her husband approved of her extracurricular activities, but there were always whispers. The whispers were that he'd had plenty of his own affairs. What you saw on the outside, though, was more of a facade than it was reality.

Ricky had always had those special customers that he dealt with a bit differently. Not necessarily because of the job or the amount of money that they were paying him to do it, but because he actually enjoyed it. For him, it was almost like an escape from the real world. For a brief time, he could be someone other than who he really was. "Mr. Orgasm" was more than a stage name; it was a persona. When he was "Mr. Orgasm," he could do things that he wouldn't normally do for fear that it would ultimately affect his daughter. The majority of the time, he was able to control this environment. With most of the women in the club, he would be able to keep them at bay and make them understand that it didn't matter what they did when they were inside the club. At the end of the day, what happened in the club stayed in the club. With Octavia, he learned how difficult this could be with some women. It was truly a test because he wanted to control things at all times.

On one particular night when they had their alone time, as usual, he performed for her. However, this alone time wasn't inside the club. He'd been meeting with her outside of the club on his alone time. While she sat on the tufted red seat watching him intently, he danced around her while keeping his eyes on her. She was turned on watching his abs and his rock-hard dick moving along to the music. He was completely naked, not wearing any costume as he did when he performed on the main stage. She couldn't wait to feel him, but she loved watching him just as much as she did fucking him. Feeling him was just the icing on the cake.

"Damn, you're so sexy, baby," he said as he stood in front of her massaging his dick.

She smiled and licked her lips. She wanted to taste him. Inside the club, there were some limitations—but outside of the club, she could have him in any way that she wanted. There was no time limit, and he would do everything slow. Nothing about this time was rushed, and not only did Octavia enjoy this time, Ricky did as well.

The two stared at each other for a few silent seconds before he grabbed the back of her head and guided her lips to his dick. Without any hesitation, she wrapped her thick lips around it while using her tongue to massage the shaft at the same time. She moaned as she enjoyed the taste of his precome trickling down her throat.

"Ahhh, shit," he said aloud, and he thrust himself farther down her throat.

Her lips were so soft and wet that she almost sent him into an early eruption. He pulled back for a second to release himself from her grip.

"Damn, girl, what the hell are you trying to do to me?"

She laughed, knowing that she was a professional at her job. She was willing to do whatever it took to satisfy him because she wanted him all to herself. She didn't care about his job or the women that he needed to please to make a dollar. All she cared about was being the one on his arm in public. She was willing to leave her husband to make that happen.

"I'm just trying to make you feel good," she said in a sexy tone as she got up from chair and stood in front of him.

Their eyes met before she moved in closer and began to passionately kiss him. She was so turned on that she could feel her panties being soaked with warm juices. The two of them moaned while they kissed, both of them enjoying the taste. She could feel his dick poking her down below. She wanted to kiss it one more time before they were through. She backed away and stopped kissing him before getting down in the squatting position and grabbing ahold of his dick with her right hand. With her left hand, she reached down into her panties and massaged her throbbing clit. The sounds of them moaning together was enough to make anyone listening horny. She was able to deep throat every inch of him without even the slightest bit of gagging.

He'd been given head on many occasions, but there was just something about the way that she handled his dick that made it hard to contain himself. Maybe it was her many years of experience, or maybe she just was a stone-cold freak. Either way, she gave the best head he'd ever had.

After a few more minutes, he couldn't take it anymore. He needed to feel her warm walls wrapped around his dick. He backed away from her and grabbed her arm to pull her up to a standing position. He forcefully kissed her before turning her around and bending her over the chair. He grabbed ahold of her black thong underwear and ripped it from her waist. He was breathing heavily as he grabbed her right thigh from behind to rest her foot on the chair. Pushing her back to make a deeper arch, he rubbed the head of his dick along her wet pussy lips from behind. He could feel the warmth without even entering her yet. He rubbed it all up and down her clit before shoving it inside. She inhaled deeply as he pushed every inch inside. You could hear how wet she was by the sound that was made each time he moved in and out. His balls slapped against the back of her left thigh as picked up the pace. They were both out of breath, but both wanting to go as long as they could to make it worthwhile.

He backed away from her to hold in his nearing explosion once more.

"Don't stop," she said as he was fully removed from her snug walls.

"I ain't stopping; come here," he said.

She walked over to him with a huge smile anticipating what was next. There was always something different. Each time they met and had sex was never the same. No boring missionary sex would do; Ricky was more of an exhibitionist.

"Take off that dress," he said while licking his lips.

As she began to remove her dress, Ricky quickly got on his knees and began eating her pussy before she could even get the dress over her head. Her knees almost buckled from the sensation of his tongue up against her clit.

"Oh my God," she said aloud. She threw her dress to the ground and grabbed the back of his head. "I love the way you eat this pussy," she said.

He continued making circles while she screamed for joy. He was taking her body to all of the places that she needed to go. Being with him was truly a stress reliever. She could get away from all of the craziness in her world when she was wrapped up with him.

"Oh shit, I'm about to come," she screamed.

Her body began to shake as she creamed all over his face and beard. He sucked ever harder, causing her to go into two more consecutive orgasms. He'd earned his stage name 100 times over in her book. Then he lay down on the floor and pulled her down into a squatting position. She slid down on his dick with ease. From all of her gym physical training, she was fit. So she could bounce on his dick like there was no tomorrow with getting tired. He loved that about her. No matter how many positions he put her in, she was always ready and never cried that she was tired. Most of the women that he encountered would come quick and be exhausted, so Octavia gave him a run for his money.

Her ass slapped up against his legs every time she dropped low. She moved her hips in circles; she moved back and forth and even grinded up against him. She came at least two more times before he was nearing his peak.

"Oh, I'm about to come. I need you to suck it, baby," he moaned.

She got off of him quickly just as she was told, slid down, and sucked every drop of come out of him as he moaned loud enough that you could probably hear him all the way in the front lobby. She swallowed all of him as he continued to breathe heavily.

"Damn!" was all that he could say.

The two lay there on the floor for the next ten minutes trying to get themselves together. As they lay quietly, Ricky was thinking about all of the things he had to do later that day. Octavia, on the other hand, had something weighing heavily on her that she needed to tell Ricky. She was nervous because she didn't know how he would take the news. Since meeting Ricky, she'd always seen her future with him in it, but she was afraid that what she was about to say would ruin all of those dreams. She knew that she couldn't hold on to the secret any longer. It was major and would change their lives. She took a deep breath before sitting up and looking over at Ricky who was lying still with his eyes closed.

"Ricky," she said.

"Yeah," he replied while opening his eyes.

"I have something important that I need to talk to you about."

"What's up?" he asked calmly even though inside he was anything but. Any conversation that starts like that was never good.

"Well, you know how I always tell you that I'm ready to leave my husband?"

"Yeah."

"Well, now, besides the fact that I want to be with you, I finally have a real reason to walk away."

Ricky began to sit up. Talking about relationships was something that always made him uncomfortable. He didn't like the direction the conversation was going in. Sure, he loved having sex with Octavia. It was amazing, but amazing sex didn't mean that there would be an amazing relationship.

"We've spoken about this before, Octavia. You know what I do, and you know that a relationship with me is bound to end in disaster."

"I know we've talked about it many times, but sometimes things happen that will make feelings change."

"Things happen like what, Octavia? What is it that you're trying to tell me?" he said getting annoyed. He hated for someone to drag things on.

"Well, last month I missed my period, and I took a pregnancy test the other day. It was positive," she said nervously.

Ricky couldn't believe what he was hearing.

"I thought you were on birth control," he said, raising his voice. His mood had just gone from relaxed to angry. The last thing that he wanted to hear from a chick that he was just fucking was that she was pregnant.

"I am on birth control, Ricky," she said with a shaky voice.

"Well, how the fuck are you pregnant? Like I believe you did this shit on purpose, Octavia. You know damn well I don't want a relationship, and I certainly don't want a baby. I'm pissed right now," he yelled as he got up from the floor and began grabbing his things from all over the room.

"Ricky, we need to talk about this."

He continued to be silent and made his way into the bathroom with his clothes and shut the door behind him. A few seconds later the shower was turned on. Octavia got up and went to the bathroom door to enter behind him, only to find that it was locked.

Ricky was inside showering and angrier than he had been in a very long time. He didn't know what he'd gotten himself into. How could he be so stupid? he asked himself. He'd always been extremely careful, but had grown to trust her, and she'd completely fooled him. He knew that having a baby with a married woman, one that he wasn't even in a relationship with, wasn't something that he wanted. Would he be wrong for demanding that she have an abortion? With all of these thoughts running through his head, he tried to calm down somehow. He didn't want to do something that he shouldn't do that could make the situation even worse. The fact of the matter was that he didn't want a baby, and he wasn't about to act like he did, so he had no other choice but to be brutally honest and hope that she would respect his wishes.

After he was dressed and calm enough to have a discussion, he came out of the bathroom to find the hotel room empty. Octavia had left him a note on the bed which read: I would never want to be a burden or someone to cause you any unnecessary stress, so don't worry. I'll take care of it.

He balled up the small piece of paper and threw it in the trash can before grabbing his wallet, jacket, and left the room. After that night he didn't hear from Octavia for a few weeks. He hadn't bothered trying to reach out to her. He went back to business as usual. He prayed that she'd taken care of things like she'd said would.

He was glad that she was handling things like the mature woman that she was. However, he couldn't have been more wrong. Almost every night that he worked he would leave, only to find some type of damage to his car. Whether it was a flat tire, scratch marks, a broken window, and even spray paint, he knew it was her because she'd left a note every time. Each note read the same thing: I'll take care of it. *He was furious, and there wasn't any way for him to find her. He didn't know where she lived, and none of her friends had attended the club since she'd gone missing in action.*

When she finally resurfaced, she walked in as if nothing happened, head held high and sitting in her normal booth with her normal group of friends. It took everything in him not to physically put hands on her. He wasn't about to risk his freedom, though. It just wasn't worth it. After the show, he pulled her to the rear of the club. She didn't resist.

"You know you have some fucking nerve showing up in here after the shit that you did," he said in her ear. He was trying not to cause a scene by yelling, but he wanted to make sure that he got his point across.

"I have some nerve? You have some nerve to basically force me to get an abortion, and then you didn't even call to check on me."

"I didn't force you to do shit. I told you that's not what I wanted. It's a big fucking difference."

"Stop cursing at me, OK? You broke my heart. I was ready to plan a life with you."

"Listen, it's clear that you and I saw two different things in our arrangement. I'm not about to apologize for not wanting a damn baby with a married woman. You fucked up our arrangement—not me. I could've got past that shit, but then you acted like a child and fucked up my vehicle. That turned me off, and I can never look at you the same again. At this point, I'm washing my hands of this, and I pray that you can walk away like an adult this time."

She didn't utter another word. She walked away, and though she was still in attendance each week, she never spoke to him again. It was a learning experience for Ricky. It was something that he vowed to never get himself into again.

There were plenty of women sitting around with smiling faces and money in hand. There were those regulars, including Octavia, and a few newer faces that he hadn't seen before. He looked up and saw Nancy and India talking on the balcony. They were always talking business. It didn't matter what was happening on stage; you could always count on Nancy focusing on their money. He looked over at the entrance and saw Big Nook, the head of security, scanning people with his handheld metal detector. It was always comforting to see that they would be safe inside of the club. He glanced to his right and saw a group of females lined up at the bar. Seeing a bunch of women buying drinks was always a good thing. Drunk women spent money . . . a lot of it. It excited him to see women with drinks in their hands. Those were the women that he paid the most attention to. Once they had some alcohol in their systems, it was a lot easier for them to forget about their bills, their men, and anything else that they had going on in their lives. There were women of all different ages, sizes, and races standing along the wall conversing.

As his showtime neared, he began to get warm. He was ready to give all of the women the show that they desired. He wanted to give them whatever it was that they were missing at home. Every show was for women only. There were no men allowed, but that didn't stop the hustlers and ballers from parking outside the club, showing off their expensive cars, waiting patiently for the women to start pouring out the door at two o'clock closing time. The cars would be lined out in front of the club, like a celebrity car show convention. It would take almost an hour for the police to break up all the excitement and send people on their way.

Ricky continued to look out at the crowd, while all the other male dancers were in the back preparing for their group and solo performances. Each week, the twenty dancers would have a new group routine to perform and execute for their screaming fans. Afterward, they would, one at a time, perform their solo dance act. Ricky saw his young friend, DJ Twist, up on the balcony spinning the turntables. He had got his friend the job two weeks earlier, after Nancy had fired the former DJ for drinking on the job. DJ Twist had the sounds banging, and the crowd of women moving, snapping, and grooving to the music. Nancy had bought a state-of-the-art Sony system, with built-in fifteen-inch speakers all around the club. As the sounds of all of the latest dance tracks banged out of the speakers, women walked around, sipped on

Coronas and Long Island Iced Teas, and chatted amongst one another.

Ricky turned and smiled as he walked away thinking about the show that he was about to put on. Even though he had been an exotic dancer for over a year, nervousness still found a way to enter his body. He looked at the group of men as they practiced their upcoming performance. Each man had a bow tie wrapped around his neck and tight-fitting thongs that snugly covered their bulging manhood. Every one of the dancers had a handsome face and a nice body. Out of the twenty of them, twelve were black, three white, and five were Spanish. They were nineteen men with nineteen different personalities, all trying their best to be the number two dancer at the club. Ricky had the number one spot on lockdown. On his worst night, none of the others could carry his jockstrap.

Suddenly, all the lights inside the club went off. Only the fluorescent green stage lights could be seen. The crowd of women all started cheering and standing up from their seats, yelling and clapping with sure anticipation. DJ Twist turned down the loud music and spoke into the microphone.

"Are y'all ready, ladies?" he yelled.

The sound of the screaming females erupted throughout the club.

"I don't hear y'all!" he yelled.

Once again, the women inside the club raised their voices to the top of their lungs.

"Okay, ladies, stand up; get y'all asses outta those seats. It's time to get this party started!" DJ Twist yelled excitedly into the microphone.

"Introducing Philly's own exotic male dance posse, the Show Stoppers!" he announced with enthusiasm.

For the 300 screaming females, the long wait was finally over. Now it was showtime.

Chapter Two

Party Time

The lights that were positioned all around the club started flashing, as the large red velvet stage curtain slowly began to slide open. When the curtain had finally opened completely, the twenty exotic dancers all stood next to each other, facing the crowd of screaming female fans. For twenty minutes, twenty exotic dancers did a well-choreographed performance to DJ Twist's mixing and scratching. After their group performance had ended, it was time for each dancer to perform his solo act. As the dancers did their thing one by one, the women inside the club went wild. Big Nook had to personally throw six women out of the club for their outlandish behaviors. There were rules inside the club. The women weren't allowed to touch the men, they weren't allowed to come on stage, and they weren't allowed to touch the thrown money. Often, there would be some women overly drunk and acting like fools. There were always some women around that didn't like to follow the rules. They looked at these men like a well-cooked filet mignon steak, so they would go above and beyond for a chance with them. Even though the dancers fed off the attention, they were grateful that Big Nook was always there to quickly get things under control.

Big Nook was the head of security and an off-duty police officer who worked at the club. He stood at six foot seven and weighed 300 pounds, with a license to carry. He was known as the "Gentle Giant," though. Because of his massive size, people would automatically assume that he had an attitude to match. He wasn't naturally aggressive, but if you pushed him, he wouldn't hesitate to use his weight to sit your ass down. When someone would piss him off, the "Gentle Giant" would quickly turn into André the Giant and start whipping some ass.

As the music continued to blast from the speakers, the dollars filled the stage and blew in the air. Dancers would jump off the stage and into the arms of excited women, who wanted to get a feel of the goods. Once a dancer had finished his routine, his body would be covered with lipstick and handprints. His thong would either be torn apart or hidden safely in someone's purse. They would leave the stage with plenty of money, but the real money was made upstairs inside one of the small, cozy rooms. Inside of those rooms they could talk, hug, kiss, or pretty much do anything else that came to mind for the right price. Nancy charged $200 for every half hour. She took half, and the dancer got the other half. Altogether, there were seven "chitchat" rooms. The line of horny women would wait around flashing their hundred-dollar bills, hoping to be chosen by one of the exotic dancers. Some women had even managed to get inside of a few rooms before the club closed at two o'clock. When it was time for Ricky's solo performance, the stage lights started blinking. As usual, he was the last performer—the one they all had been waiting for—the grand finale!

"Okay, ladies! It's about that time!" DJ Twist shouted into the microphone. Married, single, young, old, black, white, Asian, Spanish—all the women started yelling and chanting his name in unison. "Mr. Orgasm! Mr. Orgasm! Mr. Orgasm!"

"Club Chances proudly presents the number one male exotic dancer on the planet, my man, y'all fantasy—'Mr. Orgasm!'" DJ Twist said as he released his hand from the turntable. The sound of R. Kelly's classic song "Bump N' Grind" instantly flowed from out of the speakers. When the women in the club watched "Mr. Orgasm" stroll on stage, wearing a black leather cowboy outfit, the crowd went wild. He gracefully flowed to the rhythm of the classic song. In one smooth motion, he slid across the stage on his knees and tossed his cowboy hat into the screaming crowd. Women were pushing and shoving each other out of the way to get it. Nancy and India stood on the balcony with pleased expressions on their faces. Big Nook and his team of security guards walked around controlling the crowd. Women's panties, thongs, and bills started filling the stage.

"Do your thing, you fine-ass nigga!" a woman yelled out. "Mr. Orgasm" slowly took off everything except his red thong. While undressing, he never missed a beat. The women watched as his dark brown, physically fit body did the snake across the stage.

Every time he would perform on stage, a rush of adrenaline would run through his entire body. The stage was his life. His freedom. He did his best and gave his all, making sure that the long, hard hours of dance practice would pay off. And it did. At the end of "Mr. Orgasm's" fifteen-minute solo performance, he grabbed a box of long stem roses and started throwing them into the boisterous crowd. It was his signature moment that he would do after the end of each performance. He tossed them all into the crowd except for two. The two yellow roses that he was going to give out to two special females he'd pick to escort him inside one of the cozy, private, chitchat rooms.

As DJ Twist kept the sounds coming, "Mr. Orgasm" leaped off the stage. He calmly walked through the crowd as the women pulled, touched, grabbed, shouted, screamed, and fainted. "Please pick me!" "No, me!" "I need a yellow rose!" "Me too!" were just a few pleas and bargains and propositions offered as he walked through the club. "Mr. Orgasm" finally spotted the two females that he was searching for. In the back corner of the club were two attractive twins sitting at a table. When he approached their table, he tossed them both a yellow rose. As large smiles filled their faces, he winked and turned away.

While the other dancers were talking and giving lap dances, "Mr. Orgasm" walked around the club mingling with all the ladies. He knew that most of them only wanted a good feel of his eight-and-a-half-inch dick. So he made sure he gave them all what they wanted—and paid for.

"How much for one hour with me at the Sheraton?" a dark-skinned woman asked.

"I'll pay you a hundred just to suck it!" a petite white woman shouted.

"Mr. Orgasm" just smiled, showing his beautiful white teeth, and continued on without responding. He was used to the many offers that women threw his way, but everyone knew just how picky he was. To be one of the few lucky women who was chosen to enjoy some private time together, a woman had to be rich, a total dime piece, or both of the above, combined. Ricky had a good eye for picking a woman with an extensive cash flow. It didn't always mean that they had to be dressed expensively either. It could be something as simple as an earring or the way they sat and crossed their legs. He just had a deep understanding of women and the way that they carried themselves. It was a science that only he understood.

When Nancy had walked downstairs to check on things, India remained by the balcony. Her light brown eyes followed "Mr. Orgasm" through the large crowd like a hungry hawk eyeing its prey. Just like most of the women inside the club, her panties were moist from excitement. Every time "Mr. Orgasm" would perform, he would have India caught up in the rapture of lust and passion. Her mother Nancy had known about her infatuation with him. That's why she told India to stay away from him. And she told Ricky the same thing. "Stay away from my daughter. She's not ready for a man like you. Cross the line and you'll be in the unemployment line!" Nancy would threaten. "Or worse!" she continued seriously. India never knew why her mother had forbidden her to stay away from Ricky. It was obvious that her mother was hiding something from her. But she was too afraid to ask, so she just left it alone. There was a secret that Nancy and Ricky shared; a dark secret that both had promised themselves never to expose.

"Mr. Orgasm" finally made it through the boisterous crowd of screaming females. When he reached the upstairs balcony, the first person he noticed was India. For a few seconds, their eyes locked. For that single moment in time, all the noise around them had suddenly silenced. The gentle smack on his ass brought Ricky back to reality. It was one of the beautiful twins, smiling and standing behind him. Her identical twin was already waiting by the door of the Champagne Room. Both women were dressed in black, tight-fitted V-neck dresses with no bra or panties underneath. They were two tall redbones, with long, silky black hair, and bodies like runway models. India didn't say a word. She just watched as the one twin grabbed Ricky's hand and led him over to her grinning sister. When the three of them went inside the room and shut the door, India turned back around and looked over the balcony, disappointed.

Half-drunk women were throwing money in the air like it grew on trees. Dancers were giving lap dances or taking women into the other available Champagne Rooms. Artie, the bartender, had his hands full with paying customers. DJ Twist blended hit song after hit song on the two turntables. Big Nook and his men controlled the crowd. Nancy was back inside her private office, stuffing the money she made off the door into the secret safe she had behind the large file cabinet.

India stool outside of the room unable to move. There wasn't a need for her to stand guard, but she'd often wished that she could take the place of other women in the room with "Mr. Orgasm." There were a few times that she'd even tried to listen in at the door, but the music was too loud most times to hear much of anything. She was envious of the women that would get private time with him. She'd always try her best to make it less obvious that she was there only to spy on him by always shuffling paper or keeping her phone—anything—in her hand. Anything that wouldn't make her look like a creep. She was just interested in what it was that kept them coming back week after week for more.

Inside the room, Ricky was seated in one of the plush leather chairs with both twins down on their knees slobbing all over his dick and balls. Both of them showed him equal attention. You could hear the slurping sounds mixed with their moans. While most people would be disgusted by the thought of having a threesome with identical twins, Ricky could care less. For him, this was just a paycheck, and he'd perform as if they were the only two women in the world.

After a few more minutes of oral pleasure, Ricky was back in control. The women loved to give him head, but they'd only paid for an hour of his time, and unless they planned on paying for additional time, it was time to fuck these women and get it over with. He found his mind drifting to India. He was aware of the fact that she would hang around outside of the room often while he saw his private clients. He couldn't lie about his attraction to her. There were times where he'd pictured her while he was fucking other women. It was getting harder to stay away from her, but he'd have to fight through the temptation as long as he possibly could. He shifted his focus back to the task at hand.

Grabbing a condom from the shelf, he watched as both of the twins stripped naked and got into position. Both were facedown, ass up on the bench in the center of the room. He walked up behind them and slid his dick inside of one woman while using his fingers to stimulate the other one's clit. Both women groaned almost in unison. It sounded like something straight out of a porno flick. He took turns fucking each one, all while looking at the clock. He had just a few minutes left before their time would be up. Both women had multiple orgasms, so regardless of whether Ricky himself had one, his job was still complete.

An hour after Ricky and the two twins walked out of the room, India was still standing on the balcony. She saw the look of total satisfaction in both women's eyes. It was the same look that every woman who Ricky chose would walk out with afterward . . . The look that India desperately yearned for and that caused nothing but envy in her heart. After a long sigh, she turned and walked away.

Chapter Three

After the Show

"Man, fuck that nigga! What kind of gay-ass name is 'Mr. Orgasm'? I don't know why all these fine-ass women break their necks to get up here every Monday and Wednesday!" Roscoe said seriously.

"I don't know why either. In high school, Ricky was a skinny no-game lame," Damon added, as they both started laughing.

"I know one thing, if lover boy ever try to sweet-talk my fiancée Tori, she will be the last woman he will ever do it to!" Roscoe said looking out the window of his black Cadillac Escalade. Both men sat inside the truck watching as all the women walked out of the club, very excited.

Expensive automobiles were lined up along the street. The fall night was tranquil, so a few people had their convertible tops down. The sounds of hip hop and reggae music filled the darkness of the air. The outside of Club Chances was like a party itself. Roscoe and his right-hand man Damon were known street thugs. They did everything from selling drugs, extortion, to even kidnapping. Roscoe was a dark-skinned, stocky guy with average looks. Violence was the only way he knew how to get things done. The only person who could get to his soft side was his beautiful fiancée, Tori. She was the love of his life. That's why he would spoil her with all the finer things that his dirty money could buy.

His best friend Damon was a brown-skinned guy with above-average looks. Many women found him attractive but very immature. Damon was Roscoe's "yes-man." He agreed with everything Roscoe said. When they were all students at the University High School in West Philadelphia, Roscoe and Damon were known as the two troublemakers. Once they jumped Ricky and chased him all the way home. For four long years, Roscoe and Damon had made Ricky's high school life miserable. After high school had finally ended, the next time Roscoe and Damon would run into Ricky again would be four years later, after Ricky had finished serving his country in the U.S. Marines. Now their one-time pushover was an ex-marine, who grew six inches taller and put on fifty pounds of muscle.

When Tori and her girlfriend Malinda walked out of the club, they spotted the large black truck parked right across the street. They crossed Lancaster Avenue, and both got inside. Tori leaned over and gave Roscoe a kiss on the cheek.

"Hey, baby, how long have you been waiting?" she asked.

"I just got here," he lied.

"Oh, then we're right on time," Tori smiled.

"I see you got another one of those roses!" Roscoe said suspiciously, pulling his truck off down the street.

Malinda folded her arms across her chest and sat back on the seat.

"So like I was saying, what's up with all these roses and shit? Did lover boy try to holla at you? 'Cause you know I'll fuck that fake R. Kelly wannabee up!" Roscoe said stopping his truck at a red light.

"Yeah, we'll fuck him up!" Damon barked in.

"Roscoe, will you stop trippin' for nothing! I'm engaged to you. Can't nobody on earth come between you and me, boy. 'Mr. Orgasm' gives out roses to a lot of girls; that's just a part of his act," Tori explained, putting her hand around Roscoe's neck.

"I'm just saying, why you got to be there every Monday and Wednesday night like some type of groupie?" Roscoe asked, enjoying Tori's gentle hand massaging his neck.

"Baby, I told you that it's just something to do. It's me and Malinda's personal treat to us after working in that hospital all day. So can we please change the subject? I'm tired of talking about this every time we go out to the club. I don't say nothing when you and Damon go to the clubs," Tori said with a sad expression on her gorgeous light-skinned face.

Roscoe looked into his beautiful fiancée's face and shook his head with a smile. As the light turned green, he pulled off, and no one else mentioned another word about "Mr. Orgasm" or Club Chances.

India was standing near the front entrance, watching as all the satisfied women exited the club. She stood there purposely so Ricky could see her before he walked out of the club.

Big Nook looked over at India and said, "Girl, you got it bad."

India just shook her head and smiled back. "That obvious?" she asked.

"Yup. Curiosity and a few other words is written all over your pretty young face," he said.

Big Nook was one of the few people at the club who knew about India's deep infatuation with Ricky. Once in a while, he would tease her, but it was all in fun.

When Ricky had finally appeared from out of the dressing room, he was fully dressed. He had on a thick wool sweater and a pair of faded Sean John jeans. On his feet was a pair of brown suede Tims. The two attractive twins were waiting for him at their table. When Ricky approached the smiling women, they stood up from their chairs, and each grabbed one of his arms. Before Ricky and his lovely friends walked out the door, he shook Big Nook's hand and looked over at India.

"Hi, India," he said, seeing the sad expression on her face.

"Hi, Ricky. I'll see you Wednesday night, right?" she asked, replacing the sad look on her face with a fake smile.

"For sure, beautiful," he said with a smile and gave her a wink before walking out the door with the attractive twins.

"Don't worry, India. If it's meant to be, it will happen pretty, and not even your mean-ass mother will be able to stop what's inevitable," Big Nook said before walking toward the back of the club.

India stood in the entrance and watched as Ricky and one of the twins got inside of his black BMW. Before Ricky had pulled off, he looked out the window and saw India staring at him. Ricky had liked India from the first moment they were introduced. He had thought India was one of the sweetest, most beautiful women he'd ever met. It was hard for him to keep his distance from her. She was young, educated, and sexy, all rolled up in one. Every time he looked into her sexy brown eyes, he could feel her spirit calling him toward her. But he had been warned by Nancy to "keep away from her, or else." Nancy had her reasons, and so did he. Not a day went by without Ricky ever wondering, what if?

***

When Ricky slowly pulled away, a sky-blue Lexus coupe was following close behind his car, with the other twin inside it. India let her eyes follow both cars until they disappeared into the darkness of the fall night. After a long sigh, she went back inside the club. The club workers were cleaning and putting the chairs on top of the tables. DJ Twist saw India and walked over to her. In his hands were a few albums and his headphones. "You all right, India?" he asked with great concern, seeing the distant look on her face.

"Yeah, I'm fine, Twist. Nice job," she said with a smile.

"Thanks, India. Make sure you tell your mom I'll be here early on Wednesday."

"All right, Twist. Just make sure you get home safely," she said.

When Twist saw his girlfriend's car pull up in front of the club, he said his good-byes and rushed out the door. After the workers had cleaned up the club and left, India watched Big Nook lock the door behind them. Once everyone was gone, India and Big Nook walked back into Nancy's private office.

"Girl, what's your problem?" Nancy asked, seeing the sad look on India's face.

"Nothing, Mom," India said, brushing her off.

Nancy looked at her daughter with one of those (tell-it-to-somebody-else) expressions. She knew *exactly* what India's problem was. But as long as Nancy was breathing and still alive, India would have to live and deal with it.

Chapter Four

Just the Three of Us

Twenty-five minutes later

The BMW and the Lexus pulled up and parked beside each other. Ricky and the two lovely twins got out of the two cars. The twins followed Ricky into his spacious, elegant loft. The loft was near Delaware Avenue, one of the hippest streets in all of Philadelphia that was adjacent to the Delaware River. The twins' names were Keri and Teri. They were from Trenton, New Jersey.

Ricky walked over to the built-in wall unit and shuffled through some CDs. When he found what he was looking for, he put in the CD and pressed *play*. Instantly, the smooth melodic voices of Floetry flowed out of the speakers. The loft was laid out. Wall-to-wall, tan-colored carpet, high ceiling, plants, black art, cream-colored leather sectional, and a huge plasma TV. Ricky walked over to the twins and stood between them.

"Did y'all enjoy our moment at the club?" he asked.

"Yes, we did," both twins said in unison.

"Well, that was just the appetizer. Now it's time for the main course. You get to have me all night without watching the clock," he said, grabbing each of their hands.

Ricky and the twins had a strange sexual relationship. He had met them at the club six months earlier. Since their first encounter, they would meet up every three weeks for a night, or sometime a weekend, of exciting sex. Afterward, they would pay him for a job well done.

The twins eagerly followed Ricky into the master bedroom. A king-size canopy bed sat in the middle of the floor. It was neatly made up with a thick, white quilt and four, large fluffy pillows. The large walls were covered with mirrors; even the entire ceiling. Small white speakers were situated inside the four corners of the room. Ricky had it wired so that the music being played in the living room could be heard crystal clear in the bedroom as well.

"Would y'all like something to drin—?"

"No!" the twins shouted in unison, cutting him off in midspeech. Before Ricky could say another word, the twins started getting undressed. They both slid their dresses to the floor and stepped out of them. They stood side by side with their beautiful, naked bodies next to each other.

As Ricky stood there with a pleased smile on his face, the twins started undressing him. When they were finally finished, they walked over and climbed on the large bed. Everywhere they looked around, they could see a reflection of themselves in the wall-covered mirrors.

Ricky's body was like a work of fine art. And both women were totally pleased. Keri laid Ricky back on the bed, and the two of them began passionately kissing. While their lips and tongues were locked in a sensual dance, Teri gently grabbed Ricky's hard, long dick and invited it into the deepness of her warm, wet mouth. Teri made love to Ricky's dick nice and slow, sending a flow of chills all throughout his body.

As soon as Teri finished her erotic performance, she and Keri switched positions. Now Keri would finish up the wonderful job that her identical twin started. Teri straddled herself on Ricky's face, while her sister continued to please him orally. Ricky took Teri's pussy lips into his mouth and immediately found the doorway to her sensitive clit. She held on to the headboard, while Ricky's magical tongue maneuvered all around her clitoris. He reached under a pillow and grabbed a magnum condom; then he tossed it to Keri, who was still performing and giving a wonderful blowjob.

Ricky had his arms wrapped around Teri's legs as his mouth made love to her pussy lips. She gripped the headboard, staring at herself in the mirror while Ricky ate her pussy like it was the last meal of his life. After Keri had finally finished, she put the condom on Ricky's still hard dick. After it was on, she climbed on his body, in the reverse cowgirl position. She slid Ricky's rock-hard dick into her wet walls. Keri started riding the magnificent love stick nice and slow. Every time she went down on it, it felt like the head of Ricky's dick was touching her stomach. And that was just the way she liked it.

The twins had their backs rubbing against each other. One was riding a mammoth dick, while the other one had a satisfying tongue massaging her clit. The moans and grunts from both women started filling the air. Ricky lay back on the bed satisfying both women at the same time.

"Ahhh! Yes!" Keri moaned out, as she slid up and down his dick.

"Ohhh! Yhhhh!" Teri yelled out, as Ricky's tongue brought her trembling body a powerful orgasm.

"I'm com . . . com . . . commiinng too!" Keri screamed out as an orgasm swept through her trembling body. Then Keri's body slumped down to the bed. Hard breathing began escaping her nose and mouth. Ricky lifted up

Teri's body and laid her beside him. He rolled her over and placed both of her legs on top of his broad shoulders. With his still rock-hard dick, Ricky slid it inside of her pussy as far as it could go. As he performed long, hard strokes, Teri moaned with joy and pain. Keri sat there playing with her pussy, watching as her twin sister got her brains fucked out.

"What's my name?" Ricky yelled out.

"'Mr. Orgasm? Mr. Orgasm! Mr. Orgasm!'" Teri shouted out. "Oh God! 'Mr. Orgasm,' I'm com—coming again!" she cried out.

Ricky paid her cries no mind. He was like a man possessed with lust and passion.

"Please! I . . . I . . . ca . . . can't go no more!" Teri screamed as another intense orgasm ran throughout her trembling body. Her sister Keri sat on the bed with a look of total disbelief on her pretty face. Right there in front of her own eyes, she watched her sister scream, beg, and yell in pure ecstasy.

"Ahhh! Oh! Yea! Yes! 'Mr. Orgasm!'" Teri screamed out before she finally blacked out and slumped down on the bed.

Ricky looked down at his sexual prey and smiled. Then he turned and looked over at Keri. "You ready?" he asked as he crawled his naked body toward hers.

Keri looked at her unconscious sister and just shook her head. "I want the same thing you gave to my sister!"

"Don't worry, beautiful, you're gonna get every single bit," he said as they started passionately kissing. After their long fiery kiss, Ricky lifted Keri's body and carried her over in front of the large wall mirror. He stood his body behind hers, then spread her legs wide apart. Keri put both of her hands on the mirror. In one smooth motion, Ricky slid his hard dick inside her wet pussy. He tightly gripped her hips and started giving her long, thunderous strokes. She held on to the mirror for support as his magnificent dick fucked her hard from behind.

"Oohhh! Ahhh!" Keri moaned and grunted at the same time. Ricky turned her around and scooped her into his muscular arms. Once again, their lips met with a long, steamy kiss. He set her back up against the mirror still stroking away. Then he softly kissed around her neck. Keri held on tightly as Ricky carried her body around the bedroom, stopping at every mirror along the way. The sweat dripped from both of their naked bodies.

"Ohhh! Yes! Waaa!" Keri yelled out in pleasure.

Teri finally lifted up her head and looked into the mirror in the headboard. When she saw Ricky holding her sister up in his arms, she just smiled and shook her head. She stood up from the bed and walked over behind Ricky. While Ricky continued to fuck her sister, Teri kissed on his back, ass, and legs.

"Ohhhh! Right there!" Keri whimpered softly.

"What's my name?" Ricky demanded, pushing his dick in as far as it could go.

"'M . . . M . . . Mr.! Mr. Or ahhh Orgasm! Mr. Orgasm!'" she screamed out as tears of joy and pleasure fell from her satisfied eyes. "I . . . I . . . I'm coming! 'Mr. Orgasm!' I'm com . . . coming, 'Mr. Orgasm.' Yes! Yes!" Keri continued screaming, as they both climaxed at the same time.

Ricky carried Keri's body over to the bed and laid her down. Her body was trembling from the powerful orgasm that she was still feeling. Teri joined them on the bed. She watched as Ricky reached under the mattress and took out two pairs of handcuffs. He cuffed Keri to one of his hands and Teri to the other.

"Tonight, ladies, we will be one," he said, lying in between both women. As the night went on, Ricky would make love to the twins over and over again. It would be the best sex that any of them had ever had. It was well worth paying the extra thousand dollars to see Ricky outside of the club. To most, the price would be too steep, especially for sex. Sure, sex was easy to achieve, but *good* sex was something altogether different. You could search for miles before finding a man that could give you a mind-blowing orgasm, and even if you did, it still wouldn't compare to what Ricky could give. For all of the ladies that paid for his time, it was money well spent while experiencing the most powerful orgasms they would ever know.

Chapter Five

Daddy's Little Girl

Tuesday morning

The early-morning sun shined through the open window. Ricky opened his eyes and saw the two beautiful women peacefully sleeping. The three of them were all still handcuffed together. Ricky looked at the built-in clock inside the headboard and noticed the time was 7:05. He needed to drive to his parents' house and pick up his daughter Asia for school. His mother would watch her on the nights that he worked at the club. He never missed a day, and he was never late.

Ricky quickly woke up the two sleeping beauties and took off their handcuffs. Together they all got out of bed and rushed into the large, walk-in shower. As the warm water fell down their naked bodies, the two women happily washed Ricky down with liquid soap. As the water rinsed the soap off of his body, Teri got down on her knees and blessed Ricky with a fulfilling blowjob. After swallowing all his love juice, her sister cleaned him off, and together, they walked out of the shower. They dried each other's body off, then quickly got dressed. Keri opened her Prada purse and took out a small white envelope.

"Here you go, handsome. We'll see you in three weeks," she said, passing the envelope to Ricky. Ricky put the envelope inside his jacket pocket without looking inside of it.

After hugs and kisses, they all walked out of the loft and got into their cars. Ricky watched as the two twins drove off in the Lexus. Moments later, he started up his BMW and drove off in the opposite direction. After checking his voice messages and e-mails on his cell phone, Ricky pressed the *play* button on the CD player. He wasn't a fan of the early-morning talk shows, where celebrity gossip flooded the airwaves for ratings. Ricky had paid his young friend DJ Twist to put him together a CD of all his favorite singers: Lauryn Hill, Jill Scott, Vivian Green, Sade, Musiq, Floetry, Maxwell, Luther, and his all-time favorite, Mary J. Blige. As he drove his car through the dilapidated ghettoes of South Philly, he let the smooth voice of Jill Scott fill his soul.

A half hour later, in Wynnefield, after parking his car, Ricky went inside the house. Asia was sitting on the sofa holding her backpack. "Hey, sweetie," he said, walking over and giving her a big fatherly hug.

"Hey, Daddy. Grandmom and Granddad went back to sleep. Aunt Nicole dressed me up. She's in the kitchen," Asia reported with a smile.

"What's up, lover boy?" Nicole said, walking out of the kitchen.

"What's up, sis? Thanks for getting Asia dressed and ready," he said, grabbing Asia's hand and walking toward the front door.

"You got some money, Ricky? I'm broke," Nicole said. "You know it's hard for us college girls," she added. Ricky reached inside his jacket and took out the white envelope. When he opened it, he saw five crisp, new, hundred-dollar bills. "Here," he said, passing Nicole one of the bills.

"Thank you," she said, a bright smile on her face.

"Tell Mom and Dad that I'll see them later," he said, opening the door.

"All right, but we need to talk too," Nicole said, following Ricky and Asia out the door.

"What now?" he grinned.

"My professor, Ms. Langston, keeps asking about you." Nicole smiled.

"I'm gonna have to go up to the community college and come check this woman out," Ricky said, getting inside his car.

"I'm telling you, Ricky, she's cute, and she's been asking about you ever since she saw you dance and found out that you're my brother."

Ricky put Asia's seat belt on and started up the car. Nicole stood there waiting, holding the hundred-dollar bill in her hand. Ricky rolled down the window and stuck out his head. "Tell your professor that I'm sorry that I don't remember her, but just for you, Nicole, I'll drive by your school on Thursday to meet her," he said.

"Bet. 'Cause I'm having a hard time in psychology, and I need all the help I can get," she said.

Ricky shook his head and slowly drove off down the street. Nicole was his eighteen-year-old younger sister and a freshman at the Community College of Philadelphia. She was an attractive, brown-skinned female with a sharp tongue and a sassy attitude. Ricky did his best to keep her on the right path. They were as close as any siblings could be.

Nicole's young girlfriends had a crush on her older brother. She knew that most females were money-hungry gold diggers, looking for great sex and a future baby daddy. But when it came to her handsome, older brother, Nicole wasn't having it.

Ricky looked over at his beautiful six-year-old daughter and playfully pinched her cheek. “Daddy!” Asia blushed.

“You missed me, sweetie?” he asked, pulling his car up at the red light.

“Yup. Always,” Asia said with a smile.

“Hey, hey, hey, what I tell you about that?” Ricky said as he pulled off after the light changed.

“I’m sorry, Daddy. Yes, I missed you a lot,” Asia said, correcting herself. Ricky glanced over at his daughter and shook his head. Asia was a younger version and spitting image of her beautiful mother who had died while giving birth to her. Asia had hazel-colored eyes and a caramel-tone skin complexion. Her silky, black hair was fixed up in two long, braided ponytails.

“Daddy, can I hang out with Ms. India again one day?” Asia asked.

“You like Ms. India, huh?” Ricky asked, turning down the music on the CD player.

“Yeah, she’s real nice, Daddy. We had a lot of fun at the zoo last week,” Asia smiled.

“The next time I see Ms. India, I’ll ask her if she would like to take you out again. I’m sure she’ll do it because Ms. India likes you a lot too,” Ricky said, pulling the car up in front of the school yard full of playing children.

“Thank you, Daddy. I’ll see you after school,” Asia said, snatching off her seat belt and giving him a hug and a kiss.

“I love you, sweetie,” Ricky said, looking into her beautiful eyes.

“I love you too, Daddy,” Asia said, getting out of the car.

Ricky watched as Asia walked over to her teacher. After she and her teacher waved good-bye, Ricky waved back and slowly drove down the street.

After turning the volume back up, he headed for his next destination: Carmen’s.

***

When India had returned home that night, she went upstairs into her bedroom and shut the door. After getting undressed, she lay naked across her queen-size bed and thought about Ricky. India and her mother Nancy lived together in a beautiful five-bedroom home in the Chestnut Hill section of Philadelphia. After India had graduated from Howard University, with a degree in business management, she decided to move back in with her mother and help her run the club. That was a year earlier, when she had first seen Ricky. He was one of the most handsome men she had ever laid eyes on. And now she was his boss. When Nancy saw the infatuated look in her daughter's eyes. She quickly brought it to a stop.

"You stay away from Ricky, you hear me?" Nancy warned her that day.

"Mom, why?" India questioned.

"Because I said so, and besides, he's too mature for you, and he'll just end up breaking your heart," Nancy said seriously.

"Mom, I can handle myself."

India knew that there was more to it, but she didn't want to get into it with her mother. After a while, she and Ricky had become friends from working together. But whenever Nancy would spot them laughing or talking together, she would somehow find a way to break it up. *Is Mom being overprotective? Or is she hiding something?* India would often ask herself. One thing for sure, India couldn't get Ricky out of her system. And the more her mother tried to keep them apart, the more India wanted him.

Chapter Six

The Bold and Beautiful

The short trip to City Line Avenue didn't take Ricky long at all. He parked his BMW inside a parking lot and walked across the street to the Executive Suites apartments. When he entered the elegant building, Ricky took the elevator to the fourth floor. Standing in the doorway of her apartment was Carmen. Carmen invited Ricky inside and closed the door. Without any words said, she quickly grabbed his hand and led him into the spacious master bedroom.

"Where's Hardrock?" Ricky asked.

"On tour with a few other Def Jam artists," she said, taking off her Victoria's Secret bra and panties.

"He'll be gone for a month."

Ricky stood there in silence as she approached him. In his head, hearing he'd be gone for a month sounded like a cash register. Anytime that Carmen was allowed freedom was time that he could make a profit. He was always eager to get paid whenever he could. After Carmen gave him a soft kiss on the lips, she stooped down on her knees.

"How was the show last night?" she said, unbuckling his belt.

"It was nice," he answered.

"I heard. So who were the twins you gave the yellow roses to?"

"How do you know about that?" he asked with a smile.

"Come on, 'Mr. Orgasm,' you know us girls can't keep our mouths closed. I didn't have to be there. My girlfriends were there," Carmen said sliding down Ricky's jeans and boxers.

"They are just a few friends of mine. Just like you," Ricky said, feeling Carmen's soft hands rubbing his hard dick.

"I can still remember when you first gave me my yellow rose," she said, teasing the head of his dick with her lips.

Ricky looked down at Carmen as she slowly rolled her tongue over her upper lip. Carmen was sexy, and she knew it.

"You know what's so damn sexy about you?" she asked softly.

"No, what?"

"Your cool-ass demeanor. I'm sure a man like you arouses many women's interest. And the sex is just on another level. Sometime I can't stand you," she said jokingly.

"Why's that?" Ricky said, playfully.

"Because I got everything in the world that I need. Money; a rich, superstar boyfriend; jewels; clothes; and I still can't get you out of my system. And I can't keep this pretty black dick from my mouth," she revealed, opening her mouth and taking his dick inside. Ricky stood there as Carmen used her mouth to make slow, passionate love to his dick. When it came to giving blowjobs, she was truly the best who had ever done it. While Ricky's dick touched the back of her throat, Carmen massaged his balls. He stood there with his eyes closed, lost in Carmen's pleasing oral performance.

Carmen Lewis was once one of the top video models in the rap music industry. She had over twenty-five videos to her credit. She stood at five foot eight and weighed 135 pounds. Her perfect measurements, 38-26-38, drove men, and even some women, wild. Besides her beautiful hourglass figure, she had a golden-honey complexion and a gorgeous face. At twenty-three-years-old, Carmen had everything a woman would ever need. After meeting her fiancé, MC Hardrock, one of the top rappers/producers in the music industry, Carmen was quickly swept off her feet. They had met at one of Hardrock's video shoots. Two months later, they were engaged, and Carmen decided to retire from the video industry.

Hardrock was a twenty-eight-year-old gangster rapper from North Philly. He had a dark-skinned complexion on his stocky five-foot-nine frame. Just like most rappers in the music industry, he had more bark than bite. In his songs, he would constantly rap about guns, murder, sex, and violence. But 90 percent of his raps were all lies and a lot of hype. Still, the 2 million fans that had bought his first album, *Kill Or Be Killed,* idolized Hardrock and believed every single word he spit out of his platinum-filled mouth.

When Carmen felt Ricky's body tremble, she sped up her pace. Her warm, wet mouth slid up and down his dick, while her hand continued to massage his balls. When she felt Ricky's whole body jerk, she gripped his dick with both hands and prepared herself for the creamy eruption. Ricky grabbed the top of her head as he exploded his thick, creamy juice inside of her mouth. Carmen swallowed it all down without wasting a single drop on the carpet.

"I hope you still got some energy left," she said, standing up and walking over to the dresser. She grabbed a Magnum condom from off the dresser and walked back over to him. Ricky's dick was still hard when she put it on. Carmen turned around and bent over. She used the bed to support her position.

"We have plenty of uninterrupted time to spare," she said seductively.

"So are you ready to be spontaneous?" Ricky asked, grinding his dick on her phat, round ass.

"It's lubricated, so, do you, boo!"

In one smooth motion, Ricky slid his eight-and-a-half-inch dick inside of Carmen's tight asshole.

"Ohhh!" she grunted, as he started stroking in and out of her ass. Ricky gave her long, thunderous strokes, making sure every motion counted. Carmen held on to the bed with her eyes closed, enjoying every single inch of his hard dick.

"Ahhh! 'Mr. Orgasm!' Ahhh! 'Mr. Orgasm!' Ahhh! 'Mr. Orgasm!'" she moaned in ecstasy. As Ricky continued to fuck Carmen from behind, tears of total satisfaction fell from her eyes. In less than ten minutes, she was enjoying the amazing feeling of a wonderful anal orgasm.

"I'm coming! 'Mr. Orgasm,' I'm coming!" Carmen cried out as the wonderful feeling swept throughout her trembling body. When Ricky finally pulled his dick out, Carmen's naked body slumped down on the bed.

After they made love again, they took a shower together. There were many things wrong with this relationship because it was leading into territory that he vowed he wouldn't go into. But, it was comfortable, though. It was a release from all of the ones that were strictly a job. As Ricky sat on the edge of the bed tying up his shoelaces, he could smell something cooking. It was customary for Carmen to fix him a nice meal after he laid the pipe properly. He grabbed his cell phone off of the bed to see if he had any missed calls or messages before he went on about his day.

"The food is ready," Carmen yelled from the kitchen.

Ricky got up and headed toward the kitchen.

Carmen had made him a delicious egg and cheese omelet with a large glass of orange juice. They sat and talked about what was going on in each other's lives.

"So what's up with you and your fiancé? Anything new?" Ricky asked as he took a bite of eggs.

"Nothing new. I'm just bored. He gives me the world financially, you know that. I love him to death, but I always feel like I'm nothing more than arm candy when he needs to keep up with appearances. I sit up in this house all the time while he's out doing his thing."

"Well, have you told him that you'd like to do more? I mean, if you just accept it without voicing your feelings, you can't expect anything different," Ricky said before taking a sip of his juice and a few more bites of his food.

"Of course I have, but he's in his own world. You know how that can go. He doesn't show me any attention, whether it's in the bedroom or just in general. In the bedroom, no one compares to you," she laughed.

"Well, we know that, but why do you stay?" he asked. He'd finished eating his food by this point. He slid his empty plate over to her.

"Because he's all I know. What else am I going to do?" She got up from the table to place his dish into the sink.

"Come sit back down," he said.

Carmen walked back over to the seat at the kitchen table. Ricky put his hands on top of her hands.

"You are an amazing woman, Carmen. You can do anything in this world that you want to do. You have learned your own worth and should demand that you be treated the way that you deserve. If he really loves you, he'll come around. Trust me," he said.

"I truly appreciate that, Ricky. You've been an amazing friend, and I will forever be grateful for your listening ear and the attention that you give me. You're always there just when I need you," she said with a smile and a quick squeeze of his hand.

Carmen considered Ricky a good friend and a wonderful listener. As much as they were attracted to each other, they both knew that their relationship could never be more than sex. They had a mutual understanding. They were two consenting adults who played the game of sex without any of the nagging strings attached.

"I got something for you," Carmen said before Ricky stood up and was ready to leave.

"I know you said I don't have to pay you anymore, but here," she said, passing Ricky a white envelope.

"Consider it another gift from me," she smiled.

"I told you, Carmen—"

Carmen put her finger to his lips and stopped him midspeech. "Ricky, what you do for me is more than I can ever ask for. And I'm not just talking sexually. I'm talking about whenever I need a shoulder to lean on or a friend to cry to, I can always count on you. I know you don't want to be a dancer all of your life, plus you have to take care of that pretty little daughter you got. We both know that when you eventually find that soul mate that you always tell me about, that our little fling will come to an end. Don't worry about the money; you know I have access to plenty. Just promise me one thing," she said seriously.

"What's that?" Ricky asked, looking into her watery eyes.

Sighing, Carmen said, "That no matter what happens with our lives, that we will always be friends." With that, the tears started falling down her face. Ricky walked up to Carmen, and they gave each other a long, affectionate hug.

"I promise you, Carmen. You'll always be my friend," he said sincerely.

After a soft kiss on the lips, Carmen watched as Ricky walked out of the apartment and shut the door. She went over to the window and watched him get inside of his BMW and drive off. After he had disappeared, she grabbed her Gucci jacket and purse and walked out the door. When she got inside her pearl-colored convertible Jaguar, she dropped the top, put on her matching Gucci frames, and sped off. As she headed toward the King of Prussia Shopping Mall, the wind blew through her long, black hair and the sounds of Lil' Kim banged out of her speakers.

"Hello," Carmen said answering her cell phone.

"Baby, it's me, Hardrock," a raspy voice said. "Where you been. I've been calling all morning."

"I've been busy getting my daily workout in. What's up?"

"I just wanted to call and tell you that they added a few more cities on the tour, so I'll be on the road for a few more weeks."

"Do you, boo. I'll be all right," she said.

Chester, PA, right outside of Philly

The terrified woman stood there crying while Roscoe had his .45-caliber pistol stuck down her throat. Her eyes were swollen and nose and mouth both bleeding from the brutal beating that Roscoe had just given her. The tears fell down her brown-skinned face. Her name was Robin, and she was a nineteen-year-old runaway from D.C. Roscoe would use her to sell drugs, prostitute, and set up people for him to kidnap. She was like his personal slave.

"Bitch, I told you about bringing me short money! If I come back over here one more time and my money ain't right, I'ma beat your ass worse than I did today. You hear me?" Roscoe yelled angrily.

Robin nodded her head as she cried. He took his gun from out of her mouth and kicked her to the floor.

"Clean yourself up, bitch. You got my drugs and pussy to sell! I'll be back in a few days!" he said, walking out of the house. When Roscoe got inside of his big black Escalade, Damon was already inside waiting for him.

"Man, I had to leave. You was beating the shit out of that bitch!" Damon said laughing. "Man, you hard on them bitches!" he concluded seriously.

"See, you can't play with them bitches, homie. I don't love none of those hoes. A bitch can't do nothing for me but make me my money! Love is for suckas! And I'll never be a sucker for love!" Roscoe said laughing. "Only one bitch got an invitation to my heart, and that's my fiancée Tori. And she so strung out over this dick and all the money that I give her, she ain't never gonna fuck up!" he laughed with confidence. "I don't understand how niggas get weak over them bitches, how a nigga can cry over a no-good bitch. One thing for sure, Damon, a bitch will never break me, 'cause I'm a man who can't be broken. And I don't have no weaknesses," he bragged, pulling his truck on the expressway.

"You got those X-pills ready?"

"Yeah, they bagged up and ready to go," Damon said.

"Good, 'cause pretty boy left me another message on my voice mail. He's ready again," Roscoe said smiling.

"Man, stop trippin' and light up that Haze. I told you the nigga is cool. Chill out."

Inside Nancy's private office, she was seated at her desk talking to a man.

"Did you think about the $30,000 offer?"

"I'm still thinking. I'll let you know real soon," he said.

"We did it before. This one will be a lot easier. We'll both benefit," Nancy said smiling.

"I have to go meet somebody. We'll talk about it later tonight," the man said, winking his eye and smiling, walking out of her office.

Nancy stood up from her desk. She walked over to the file cabinet and took out a manila folder with a few white sheets of paper inside of it. After walking out of her office and locking the door, she sat down at an empty table and called Big Nook over.

Chapter Seven

The Eyes of Hate

Tuesday afternoon

After Ricky left the bank, he got back into his car and headed to the club for dance practice. While at the bank, he deposited a thousand dollars into his personal account and the same amount into the account he had set up for his daughter, Asia. At least three days out of a week Ricky would do this. He had dreams of one day owning his own house, with a few acres of land surrounding the property. The money he would put into Asia's account was to ensure that if anything happened to him, she would be set for life.

On his way toward the club, Ricky picked up DJ Twist on the corner of Fifty-second and Market street. As usual, DJ Twist was waiting patiently for Ricky's arrival. If there was one thing that he could bet his last dollar on, it was that Twist would be on time. Twist was always dependable and someone that Ricky could count on in any situation. In fact, he was one of the most punctual people Ricky knew. Ricky didn't have any qualms about recommending him for a job at Chances, or anywhere else, for that matter. He'd recommended him for several different events, and he'd never heard anything negative about him. The two men shook hands as DJ Twist got into the car. Not much was said after he entered, proving how comfortable the men were in each other's presence. Ricky turned his radio up, then glanced in his side-view mirror before pulling away from the curb and making a right on Fifty-second Street.

Ricky and DJ Twist had met five years earlier at a local DJ competition. Back then, Ricky was a party promoter, and it was always good to see what DJ was the hottest in the city. The competition had all of the local DJs, including some that were from other cities in the tristate area. All of them were extremely talented. Some of them were capable of doing tricks Ricky never seen before, while effortlessly blending tracks together. DJ Twist was one of those with special tricks up his sleeve. He did one move where he spun in circles and changed the track so fast that it sounded like one song. There was no surprise when he came in first place.

Ricky was so impressed with DJ Twist's turntable skills that he hired him to become his personal DJ. He used him for every event that he hosted. After speaking with Twist and being around him as often as he was, the two became friends. Twist was loyal and trustworthy. Those were just two of the qualities that he had. There was a time when after an event a few men approached Ricky about a woman he'd been seeing. For them, it was the perfect time to approach him since he was alone. Without warning, Twist came from the rear with his gun drawn, forcing the unarmed men to back off. Ricky knew at that moment, he was someone that he definitely needed to keep around. After Nancy had fired the former DJ for drinking on the job, Ricky had gotten his young friend the vacant position.

"I made you a new CD, Ricky," Twist said, digging into his large Nike sports bag, filled with CDs, records, and his DJ accessories. "You're gonna love this one! Can I ask you something, Ricky?" Twist said with a serious look on his face.

"Yeah. What is it?" Ricky said, turning down the music.

"What's up with Nancy?"

"Why you ask me that?" Ricky said, curiously.

"Because it seems like she got something against you. What's up with that?" Twist questioned.

"It's a long story, Twist. One that I wish to forget about," Ricky said seriously.

Twist got the message and quickly changed the subject. "Okay, then, lover boy, what's up with you and India? I ain't crazy. Even a blind man can see the attraction y'all both have for each other.

"I saw India last night standing by the door watching you leave the club with the two honeys on your arm. I'm telling you, Ricky, pain was written all over her pretty face. How come y'all two ain't never hook up?" Twist asked.

"We're friends. You know she took my daughter to the zoo, and once in a while, we talk about things going on at the club. Plus, you know it's not a good idea to mix business with pleasure," Ricky said, stopping his car at a red light.

"Save it for the birds! If I had a young, fine shorty sweating me like India, I would just have to take my chances," Twist said. "Everybody at the club wants to knock shorty's boots, but the only person she show any kind of interest in is you. She's young, beautiful, and educated. What is you waiting for?"

"I don't know, Twist," Ricky said, pulling off after the light changed. "If it's meant to be, it will happen."

"Ricky, you're my man, and I got plenty love for you, homie, but women like India don't stick around too long. Niggas snatch that kind up real quick! I know you got more than enough women that you can call on, but if you ask me my opinion, Ricky, you can't go wrong with India," Twist said seriously.

Ricky just calmly nodded his head as he continued to drive.

Everything Twist said was right. Ricky did have plenty of women that he could call on, but at the same time, there was so much that Twist didn't know about him and the women who paid him just to sex them. None of them were women he'd deal with otherwise.

When Ricky pulled his BMW up in front of the club, all the other dancers' cars and trucks were parked outside. Across the street from the club, Ricky and Twist noticed Flex, Ricky's number one competitor, standing beside Roscoe's Cadillac Escalade talking to him.

"That dude Roscoe ain't nothing but trouble!" Twist said, grabbing his sports bag and getting out of the car.

"Ain't none of them dudes cool, Flex or Roscoe," Ricky replied, grabbing his black leather sports bag from off the backseat and getting out of the car. Ricky saw Roscoe pass Flex a small brown paper bag. When Flex put the bag inside of his jacket pocket, Roscoe rolled up the truck window, and he and his friend Damon sped off down the street.

"What's up?" Flex said walking across the street.

Both Ricky and Twist just nodded their heads. Flex was an ass-kissing backbiter that only a handful liked. Ricky was not one of them. A few times they had almost come to blows. After Ricky "Mr. Orgasm" Johnson, Flex was the next most popular exotic dancer at the club. Flex stood at six foot three, 185 pounds, and had a light complexion and a perfect physique. A few tattoos covered his muscular arms and back. Flex was a twenty-five-year-old pretty boy with an ugly attitude. His light hazel eyes and short black, curly hair would drive the women wild and crazy. His conceited, arrogant, stuck-up attitude didn't keep them around for long, which is why Flex couldn't get the number one exotic dance position at the club. Ricky was a much-better dancer with better skills. Whenever Ricky would perform his routine, he *owned* the stage. In his routine, he'd fly through the air or slide across the stage doing all kinds of acrobatics. This too would drive the women crazy. Ricky enjoyed performing for all his female fans. Seeing them smile, clapping, and screaming his name would always bring a smile to his heart. Flex was the total opposite. He only cared about three things: money, who he could sex, and the day he would get Ricky's number one exotic dance title.

When Ricky and Twist walked into the club, everyone was standing around inside. Nancy and Big Nook were seated at a table going over some paperwork. A few dancers were on the stage already practicing their routines for the next show. India was sitting alone at a table keying something in on her laptop computer.

After Twist had gone upstairs to his DJ booth, Ricky walked over to India and sat down in an empty chair.

"What's up, pretty? What are you doing?" he asked.

"Hi, Ricky. Soon, we'll have a winner for your ultimate fan contest," she said. "You have a lot of female admirers e-mailing you."

"Will I be able to see a picture of the winner?"

"Nope. Sorry," India smiled.

"Oh, well, maybe I'll be lucky."

"I see everybody wants a piece of 'Mr. Orgasm,'" India said.

"I guess," Ricky said softly.

"What's wrong? Ain't that what you want?" India asked seriously

"Sometimes I do, and sometimes, India, it can be one big headache. For real, all I want is my own dance studio one day and a nice big house for me and Asia to live in," he said with a serious expression on his face.

"What about that special someone to share your quality time with? Every man needs a good woman by his side."

"Maybe one day I'll find her. I'm very picky."

"I noticed," India retorted. "How's Asia doing?" she said, quickly changing the subject.

"Fine. She asked about you this morning. She really likes you," Ricky smiled.

"I like her too. She's such a beautiful little girl. Honestly, I can't wait to have my own child one day," India said, closing her laptop.

"Girl, you're way too young to be thinking about having children," he said playfully.

"Ricky, believe it or not, I'm old enough for a whole lot of things and anything that I don't know, I'm willing to learn with the right teacher," she said seriously.

Before Ricky could respond, Nancy approached the table.

"First of all, you're late; second, you're bothering India while she's working," Nancy said in an angry tone.

"Mom, he wasn't bothering me. We were just talking about his fans on the Web site," India said defensively.

"I'm sorry, Nancy, that I was late, but I had to go pick up Twist. Thanks for everything, India, we'll finish this conversation some other time," Ricky said, grabbing his bag and walking away.

When he left, India looked up at her mother and said, "Mom, why do you always do that when Ricky comes around? He's your number one exotic dancer, and you treat him like he's nothing. Why don't you run Flex or the other dancers off when they come to talk to me? Why is it Ricky?" India asked seriously.

"I don't have to explain nothing to you. You just stay away from Ricky, and that's that!" Nancy said, walking away.

When Nancy walked by Ricky, he saw her eyes filled with hate and rage. He watched her walk into her office and slam the door. Ricky looked across the room at India and shrugged his shoulders. He saw the confused look on her face and just shook his head. India knew that sooner or later she and Ricky would have to talk. It was killing her to keep her emotions suppressed. If Ricky didn't come to her soon, then India had already decided to go to him. She could hardly sleep at night thinking about Ricky. So whatever the problem between her mother and Ricky was, India was now more determined to find out the answer.

Chapter Eight

If Only They Knew

When dance practice ended, everyone packed up their belongings and left the club. India was so upset with her mother that she walked out of the club without saying good-bye. Ricky and Twist watched India get inside her cherry Range Rover and sped off down the street.

"Ricky, I'll see you tomorrow night," Thunder said walking toward his parked car.

"Take it easy, big boy," Ricky said as he and Twist climbed inside his BMW. Thunder was the biggest of all the male dancers. He stood at six foot five and 275 pounds. He had a light brown complexion. He kept his hair cut low, sporting a head full of waves. Out of all the dancers at the club, Thunder was Ricky's closet friend. After Thunder got into his Hummer H3 and drove off, Ricky pulled off right behind him. Ricky had to drop Twist off at home. Then afterward, he had to go pick up Asia at her school.

Nancy, Flex, and Big Nook were the only people left inside the club.

"Nancy, I'll see you tomorrow evening," Big Nook said, grabbing his bag off a table.

"Make sure you and your boys get here an hour earlier. You know how Wednesday nights are. I want y'all to set up before all those horny-ass women start kicking the door down," she said, walking Big Nook to the front door.

"Don't worry, we'll be here," Big Nook replied, walking out the door without saying a word to Flex. Big Nook didn't like Flex at all. Flex felt the same way. So the two of them just kept their distance. After Big Nook had gotten into his car and driven off, Nancy locked the door. Flex followed her back into her office. As soon as she shut the door, she started taking off her clothes.

"Do you think Big Nook knows about us?" Flex asked, undressing.

"Maybe he suspects something's going on between us, but he's a cop; that's his job," Nancy said while taking off her bra.

"What about Ricky? He knows a lot. Do you think he'll ever blow the whistle?" Flex continued to ask.

"Flex, no one knows the whole truth about you and me. Ricky is old news. Our little affair ended right before my daughter graduated from college and my husband's untimely death. I'm sure he's probably put the pieces together, but Ricky has moved on. Plus, he knows that he'll be as much of a suspect as you and I. He don't want no drama in his life. That little daughter of his is his world. Ricky don't want to bring no unnecessary trouble his or her way," Nancy assured him as she walked up to Flex, naked.

"So what about that number one dance spot? When can I finally get it? Since we've been messing around, I've done everything you asked me to. This club is yours because of me, Nancy," Flex said seriously.

Nancy looked into his light hazel eyes and said softly, "Flex, baby, what did I tell you before? You'll get the number one spot when the time is right. Right now, baby, Ricky is bringing in a lot of money to the club, and because of him, we are the number one exotic dance club on the East Coast. He's my money right now. I'm bringing in over $25,000 every Monday and Wednesday night with Ricky being the headlining act. You remember what happened when he got sick that time? The club wasn't even half packed," Nancy reminded him while putting her arms around his waist.

"Just be patient, give me some more time. Soon, my husband's death will be forgotten, and Ricky will be played out. Then, baby, you'll have the number one spot," Nancy assured him, kissing all over his chest. "Now, handsome, I'm tired of talking about Ricky and my late husband. I need my daily fix. I have been feening all day like a crackhead," she said, walking over to her desk and spreading her legs apart.

"So how do you want it?" he smiled.

"I want you to fuck the shit out of me. Just like you did Sunday night in the hotel. But this time when you smack my ass, don't be so damn hard," Nancy teased seductively.

Big Nook pulled his grey Crown Victoria into the Kentucky Fried Chicken parking lot and parked. Moments later, a blue Ford Taurus pulled up beside him. A short, dark-skinned man quickly got out of his car and got inside of Big Nook's.

"What's up, Nook? Find out anything yet?" he asked.

"Nothing. If she did have anything to do with killing her husband, she ain't showing it," Big Nook responded.

"What's up with her young lovers?"

"Nancy and Ricky's affair didn't last long. When he was fucking her, her husband was still alive. I'm almost positive that Ricky had nothing to do with her husband being murdered. He's a good kid; something scared him away from Nancy. Now they barely talk, because she can't stand him for some strange, unknown reason. The only reason she puts up with him is because of all the money he brings to the club. So scratch him off your suspect list. He's clean, believe me," Big Nook said.

"What about the guy Flex? As soon as lover boy pops up on the scene, her husband suddenly dies. This has 'Hollywood True Story' written all over it. Greed, lust, sex, and murder!" the man said.

"Well, right now, I don't know too much about their sexual relationship, Detective Hightower. I was hired a week before the murder happened. Maybe Nancy wanted it that way. But the day her husband Richard was murdered, I didn't work. Nancy's a sharp woman. She's no fool. Whatever is going on with her and Flex, they keep it very secret. I know what's going on because I pay a lot of attention. That's what I get paid for. Maybe Ricky knows as well, but I'm sure that no one else at the club has a clue that Nancy and Flex have been having an affair right under our noses," Big Nook said.

"Maybe you're right, but I followed them Sunday night to the Sheraton Hotel out by the airport. I waited inside my car for over two hours," Hightower laughed.

"Do you think her daughter knows?" Hightower asked.

"I seriously doubt it. India is too busy running the day-to-day operations and yearning for Ricky's attention."

"Oh yeah?"

"To be honest, I think they both want each other but are afraid to cross that line. Ricky tries not to show it, but he wants her just as much as India wants him," Big Nook said.

Hightower went inside his jacket pocket and took out a small minitape recorder. "Here," he said, passing it to Big Nook. "When you get a chance, just hit the red recorder button and hide it somewhere. This baby will pick up everything up to twenty feet away. You said that Nancy only allows you and her daughter into her office. So the next time you get a chance, make sure you hide it inside the office somewhere. The recorder has a magnet on the back that will stick to any metal. It can record up to four hours. Sooner or later, Nancy will say something she's gonna regret. If she did plot her husband's murder, then most likely she'll tell on herself. Maybe her young lover will say something incriminating. Tell the boys to keep their eyes and ears open. If Nancy's the woman that I think she is, I don't want her to get away with murder. Her type is the worst! After the rich husband gets old and needs Viagra to boost him up, they go find a young lover to get rid of him and take his place. I wouldn't be surprised if they're inside her office fucking right now. On my way over here, I saw both of their cars still parked outside," Hightower revealed zipping up his jacket.

"Yeah, I just left them before I came here to meet you," Big Nook said.

"Like I said, big fella, this has 'Hollywood True Story' written all over it," Hightower said shaking his hand and getting out of the car. Exhaling, Big Nook pulled out of the parking lot and drove off.

Chapter Nine

The Conscience of Love

After Ricky dropped Twist off at his house, he went to pick up Asia. He was always excited to spend some quality time with his daughter. His life was so fast paced that he enjoyed the time he got to slow down. His daughter was one of the smartest children he knew. He loved how he could sit and have conversations with her that most would assume were beyond her years. Her personality was special. There were nights that she kept him laughing well into her bedtime. He cherished those moments with her, and he made sure that she knew it.

After he and his daughter got to his parents' house, Ricky helped Asia with her homework. It was something he would do every day. Once they had finished her homework, he sat around talking to Asia. He would play games with her or whatever else she wanted to do before dinner. His mother would always throw down in the kitchen, so he looked forward to that meal as well as the family time.

This particular day, the two of them played a quick game of jacks before going downstairs inside the kitchen and enjoyed a delicious chicken dinner with his parents and his sister Nicole. After dinner, as they did every night, Ricky and Asia went back upstairs to her bedroom and watched her favorite cartoon on the Nickelodeon channel. Before Ricky left, he kissed her on her lips and said, "Sweetie, if you want to talk to me later, call me on my cell phone like you did before."

"Okay, Daddy, I will," she said. "Daddy, did you see Ms. India today?" she asked innocently.

"Yes, sweetie, I told her what you said. Maybe next time we can all go to the zoo together," Ricky said, sitting on the edge of Asia's bed while rubbing his hands through her long, silky hair.

"Thank you, Daddy, I love you," Asia said, wrapping her arms around Ricky's waist and giving him a big hug.

"I love you too, sweetie. Now don't forget, whenever you want to talk to Daddy, just call me," he said, kissing her forehead.

"I will, Daddy," Asia said softly.

When Ricky walked downstairs, his parents were sitting on the couch watching TV. He walked over and sat down between them. His parents had both retired from their city jobs. Now they spent their days taking care of Asia and living a good life off of their hard earned pensions.

"Have you found her yet?" his father asked.

"Not yet, Dad, still looking," Ricky grinned.

"I keep telling you, Ricky, that you can't be a playboy all your life. Ain't nothing like having that one special woman that can cure all your pains and help heal your soul," his father said, winking at his blushing wife.

"Dad, it ain't as easy as you think it is. Most of the good women is already taken, and I just don't want to settle for anybody. I want a woman who will love both me *and* Asia unconditionally," Ricky said seriously. His mother leaned over and kissed him on the cheek.

"Don't worry, I have faith in you. You'll find the right one. Now, I 'ma let you men talk. I have some laundry to take care of," she said, standing up and walking away.

"Ricky, all I'm saying is, you can't keep holding onto the past. Cheryl is gone, but she left you a beautiful daughter. A daughter who needs a motherly woman in her life," he said.

"She has Mom."

"No, Ricky, that's her *grandmother*. You and Asia both need another piece to complete your triangle of love. No matter how much your mother does for Asia, she's still just her grandmother. We are both nearing sixty. Asia needs a younger woman in her life; someone who will be a positive role model to look up to. Ricky, I know you're having a lot of fun right now, and things are going pretty well. But just think about your beautiful daughter that's upstairs inside her bedroom playing all alone with her dolls. Think about that for a second," his father said.

"But, Dad, I'm here for Asia if she ever needs anything," Ricky protested as tears welled up in his eyes.

"Son, you are a wonderful father, but your daughter needs a father *and* a mother. That's why the black family is so messed up right now. There's too much of one and not enough of the other. You might never find yourself another Cheryl, but if you continue to keep that door shut and that shield up, you might miss out on someone just as special," he said putting his arm around Ricky's shoulder.

"Dad, it's hard. Women are like vultures out there."

"What about that pretty young lady that came over here and took Asia to the zoo? She seemed really nice."

"Oh, India. We're just friends. She's the manager down at the club," Ricky said.

"Well, I saw the way she looks at you, and I'm telling you, son, the last time I saw a look like that in a woman's eyes, I ended up marrying her and having you," his father said with a proud smile.

They both stood up from the couch and walked over to the front door. After his father gave him a warm hug, he looked at Ricky and said, "While you're out there having fun, being young and energetic, don't lose sight of the big picture and never stop searching for your true soul mate."

As Ricky got into his car and drove off, he let his father's poignant words linger in his thoughts. He thought about all the women he was having sexual relationships with. The sex was good, and the money they paid him made the sex so much better. Still, deep down inside Ricky's soul, he knew something was missing.

After Ricky had gone by the gym and worked out for an hour, he took a long, warm, relieving shower and left the gym. As he drove his BMW down Walnut Street, his cell phone started ringing. He looked at the number on the caller ID.

"Hello, Gloria. What's up?" he answered.

"You, handsome!" a soft female voice said. "I miss you. What's it been, about a month now?"

"Thirty-nine days," Ricky playfully corrected her.

"Keeping count, huh?" she said.

"How can I ever forget you?" Ricky said, maneuvering his car through traffic. "You won't let me, and besides, every time we're together, it becomes a memorable occasion," he laughed.

"I'm glad you think so, because I'll be by there tomorrow morning around 10:00 o'clock. I'm bringing another bag of goodies with me," she said. "I stopped by the sex toy shop and made a few purchases."

"In that car?" he asked, shocked.

"No, I used the Mercedes," she said. "Do you like the new watch?"

"Love it; I can't thank you enough for it," Ricky said, looking at his new gold Yacht-Master Rolex watch.

"Oh yes, you can, handsome. You've thanked me way more than enough," Gloria laughed.

"Where's your husband?" Ricky said changing the subject quickly.

"His good friend Donald Trump and he took a three-day trip down to Florida early this morning."

"So when the dog goes away, the cat comes out to play, huh?" he laughed.

"Yup, especially when the cat gets to play with a younger, stronger, longer, darker dog," Gloria replied laughing. "I'll see you tomorrow morning; rest up," she said, hanging up the phone.

Ricky closed his cell phone. He set it down on the empty passenger seat. As he drove home, a big smile was on his face.

"Gloria . . . Gloria . . . Gloria . . ." he said to himself.

When Nancy had finally come home, she was so tired from her afternoon sex workout with Flex that she walked upstairs into her elegant bedroom and fell right asleep. For one intense hour, Flex had fucked Nancy all over her office. He was her young, handsome stallion. The only thing that Nancy liked old was her money. Deep down, she still wanted Ricky. Ricky was a much-better lover than Flex could ever be, but Ricky couldn't be bought or manipulated. Flex could. When Ricky realized that his affair with Nancy was wrong and deceitful, he decided to end it, leaving Nancy with unfulfilled high hopes and a wet pussy. After Ricky had abandoned the affair, Nancy became very angry and vindictive. Her love-lust romance instantly turned to one of hate and revenge. She knew that India and Ricky were very attracted to each other. If she couldn't have the wonderful "Mr. Orgasm" anymore, then neither could her daughter.

Inside her bedroom, India was lying across her bed staring at the ceiling. A few scented candles were her only source of light. She heard when her mother had walked through the door, but she didn't bother to go talk to her.

India looked over at her cell phone and thought about calling Ricky. Halfway through dialing his number, she changed her mind. She thought about all the fun she and Asia had enjoyed at the Philadelphia zoo. How surprised she was when Ricky let her take Asia. India was the only woman that Ricky had ever let Asia go with. The only other females that were involved in Asia's life were his mother and his younger sister Nicole.

India stood up from her bed and walked over to the stereo wall unit. After she pressed the CD player button, she got back in bed and lay across her silk sheets. As the smooth, soulful voice of Toni Braxton flowed out of the speakers, she reached under her pillow and grabbed the photo of her late father. She missed her father so much, wishing he was still around to take away some of her pain. When he was alive, he always did. India kissed the photo, then put it back under her pillow. Inside her cozy bedroom, she peacefully cried herself to sleep.

Chapter Ten

Trouble in the Air

Late Tuesday night

The big black Cadillac Escalade was parked right across the street from Club Chances. Roscoe and Damon sat inside the truck watching as people walked in and out of the club. Then Roscoe saw Flex walk out of the club and start walking toward his truck. When Flex approached the truck, Roscoe rolled down the window and said, “You finished already?”

“Yeah, man. They ate up those Ecstasy pills in there. I sold the whole bag!” Flex said excitedly. He went into his leather jacket pocket and took out a large stack of bills. “That’s $1,700. You got some more?”

“Plenty!” Roscoe said, going under his seat and taking out a similar brown paper bag. Flex took the bag and put it inside his jacket pocket.

“I’ll see you tomorrow night, Roscoe. Just remember, this is between us. I don’t want Nancy or Big Nook to find out. And I don’t want Ricky to find out either,” Flex said.

“Fuck Ricky! Don’t you worry about that fake-ass lover boy; you just keep doing what you do, and I’ll worry about the rest,” Roscoe said.

“See you tomorrow,” Flex said before walking back across the street.

Roscoe rolled up the window and pulled off down the road.

"I don't trust that nigga!" Damon said, passing the Haze-filled blunt to Roscoe.

"Why's that?" Roscoe asked, blowing smoke out of his nose.

"Because he knows too much. We sold him that 9 mm, and the next thing you know, Nancy's husband gets shot four times with the same kind of gun."

"So what? We ain't got nothing to do with that. If he smoked the guy, that's his business," Roscoe said, passing the blunt back to Damon.

"What if he ever told the cops that he got the gun from us?"

"His word against ours."

"What about the X-pills?" Damon asked.

"What about them? He's making us *and* himself a killing," Roscoe said, driving his truck down Parkside Avenue.

"What if he gets caught? That soft-ass pretty nigga would turn us in without even blinking!" Damon said seriously.

"Damon, you worry too much. Flex is a hustler just like us. He knows what will happen to him if he ever crosses us. This Desert Eagle on my waist will be the last thing his pretty face will ever see," Roscoe laughed. "Like I said, Damon, you don't have to worry about Flex. The motherfucker I can't stand is Ricky! He thinks the marines done made him a new man. He will *always* be that punk motherfucker we used to chase home from school!" Roscoe said as they both started laughing while they continued to drive to their next destination. The thick smoke from the blunt filled the air.

***

Tori and Malinda were standing out front of the Misericordia Hospital, where they both worked. They were waiting for Roscoe to come pick them up and drop them off at home.

"What are you wearing to the show tomorrow night?" Malinda asked, turning off her iPod.

"Maybe my white DKNY blouse, a pair of DKNY jeans, and my new leather ankle boots," Tori said, looking up the street for Roscoe's truck to appear.

"Do you think we can get one of those yellow roses off of 'Mr. Orgasm'?" Malinda asked dreamily.

"Girl, I wish! I love my baby Roscoe, but that sexy-ass nigga 'Mr. Orgasm' is one man I wouldn't hesitate to give a shot to!" Tori said with a sensuous smile.

"Me too!" Malinda laughed. "I heard that his sex is so good that he be turning women asses out!"

"Don't believe the hype! I mean, he's fine and all, but what can that nigga do that hasn't been done yet? Maybe he can turn out some of those young bitches, but with a grown-ass woman, it won't be nothing more than sex," Tori stated.

"Girl, I'm just telling you what I heard," Malinda replied.

"One thing for sure, I would still love to find out," Tori said as they both started laughing.

"What's up, DJ Twist?" a short, brown-skinned female said as Twist walked out of the restroom.

"What's up, Lexi? Having fun?" Twist asked, walking toward the DJ booth.

"Not really. I'm just about ready to go. My girl is coming by to pick me up. You know I don't mess with no drugs at all! Don't let security find out you got those X-pills in here. They're not allowed in the club. A guy who works here is selling them!" Lexi said.

"Who? What guy?" Twist asked, shocked.

Lexi scanned through the large crowd. When she saw Flex talking to two attractive young females, she said, "Him. The cute guy over there." She pointed. "Ain't he one of the exotic dancers that works on Monday and Wednesday nights?"

When Twist saw the person she was talking about was Flex, he just shook his head.

"Well, doesn't he work here?"

"Yeah, he's an exotic dancer," Twist muttered.

"Well, Mr. Exotic Dancer over there is the X-Man, and I ain't talking about the movie with Halle Berry in it. More than half the people in here have bought some e-pills from him. And he's so cute that some of the girls who don't take X still buy them off of him," Lexi said. "Twist, if you decide to change your mind, me and Lori will be outside of the club inside my car."

"No, I'm cool, Lexi," Twist said.

"Suit yourself," Lexi said, walking away through the crowd. Twist watched as Flex maneuvered throughout the club. He decided that he would only tell Ricky about Flex's new secret occupation. When the song was about to end, he hurried back to the empty DJ booth.

Chapter Eleven

Me and Mrs. Jones

Wednesday morning, 9:56 a.m.

Ricky was standing in the doorway of his loft in nothing but his white silk Gucci robe and matching slippers. With his arms crossed, he watched as the $200,000 all-black Rolls-Royce Phantom slowly pulled up and parked. The elegant car had a luxurious interior and could go from 0 to 60 in 5.7 seconds. The Phantom rolled around on twenty-two-inch specially designed rims that were imported from California.

Gloria Jones stepped out of her car. She had on a pair of tinted Dolce & Gabbana frames, a multicolored Dolce & Gabbana dress, and a pair of matching D&G strap-around sandals. Her long, blond hair was tied in a ponytail that hung down to the center of her back. At forty-nine, Gloria had a beautiful face and the body of a woman half her age. She was once one of the top models at the Ford Modeling Agency. She stood five foot ten and weighed 135 pounds. Her deep blue eyes were the color of the Pacific Ocean.

Gloria and Ricky had met at a bachelorette party six months earlier. Ever since that day when they exchanged numbers, Ricky had been Gloria's handsome, young, black secret lover. Ricky's elegant private loft, his BMW, and the new Rolex watch that he sported around were all gifts from her. None of it had made a dent in her Prada purse. Gloria was paid, loaded, big time. Her husband Larry Jones III was number 357 on the Forbes 400 list for the wealthiest 400 people in the United States. His family owned the second-largest steel company in the entire country, The Jones Steel Corporation.

Gloria reached into her car and grabbed three large shopping bags. After she shut the door, she turned around and just stood there for a few seconds, letting her blue eyes stare at her young black stallion. She slowly rolled her tongue over her upper lip. After a long sigh, she walked past Ricky and into the cozy loft. Ricky closed the door and turned around.

"How did the operations go?"

"Perfect," she said, referring to the tummy tuck and the new set of 36DD breasts her husband paid for.

"I think you're gonna really enjoy my new babies," she said with a sly smile. "Yesterday, I stopped by the sex shop on South Street and picked up a few more toys. A remote control vibrator, handcuffs, neck chokers, a whip, dildo, and a small, handheld paddle so you can spank me when I'm naughty," Gloria said with a seductive smile.

"What's in the other bags?" he asked with a grin.

"Oh, you know I can't go shopping without picking up a few items for you," Gloria said, reaching inside the white Macy's bags. She pulled out a new black leather pea coat, a red cashmere crewneck, two pairs of Gucci jeans, Prada and Versace sneakers, and Sean John, Polo, and Calvin Klein colognes.

"Gloria, I told you that you don't have to keep buying me stuff," Ricky said seriously.

"And I told you, handsome, that I don't mind. If I don't use the Black Card that I have, then what's the use of having it?" she explained, sitting down on the soft leather sectional.

Ricky sat right across from her. Gloria spread her legs apart so he could see that she wasn't wearing any panties under her dress.

"Can I ask you a serious question, Gloria?"

Gloria took off her frames and set them on the glass coffee table. "Sure, go ahead," she said, looking into Ricky's serious eyes.

"Why me? Is it just sex?"

Gloria smiled and shook her head. Then she leaned forward and grabbed Ricky's hands.

"Yes, the sex plays a major part, or else I wouldn't be risking my marriage or reputation by sneaking over here to have sex with you. Believe it or not, Ricky, every white woman wants to experience the lovemaking of a black man. Black men possess an exotic aura that no other man on earth has. When you're fucking me, I can feel your passion, pain, and desires, all at the same time. Besides the great sex, you're a handsome, sweet man, and that's why I don't mind doing all the things that I do for you." Gloria went down to her knees and started crawling toward Ricky. When she got to him, she untied his silk robe. Her body was already burning with desire. Gloria grabbed his hard dick and started teasing the head with her tongue.

"You have a lot of stuff with you, Gloria," Ricky said putting his hand on the top of her head.

"Even us rich white bitches have a dark side!" she said, as she started licking his dick like a chocolate ice-cream cone. Ricky lay back on the chair and closed his eyes while Gloria made love to his dick with her warm, wet mouth.

When India walked down the stairs, Nancy was sitting at the living-room table counting large stacks of money.

"Where are you going?" Nancy asked.

"I'm going out for a drive. I have a lot of things on my mind."

"You need a damn man in your life, and then you won't be around here stressing all the time!" Nancy said with an attitude as she wrapped a rubber band around one of the money stacks.

"Mom, please don't start with me this morning," India said, irritated.

"Why don't you come and help me count some of this money before I drop it off at the bank?" Nancy asked.

"No, thank you. Every time I look at piles of money, I think about the person who robbed and killed my father," India said angrily. "I don't know how you can take it so easy."

"I had to learn to move on. The same thing you should do, India," Nancy said.

"Sometimes I don't think I'll ever be able to move on," India said sadly.

"Well, your father left you a nice hefty fortune when he died," Nancy said with a smile.

"Mom, is all you ever think about is money?" India yelled.

"What else is there to think about?" Nancy yelled back.

"What about love? I'll take true love over money any day!" India said seriously.

"And you'll be a damn fool! Money rules the world, while true love can only be found in movies and songs."

"Money doesn't rule anything! Money is the root of all evil! Mom, one day I'm gonna find my true love and prove you wrong! I don't care if we are poor or rich; as long as we love each other, that's all that will ever matter!" India said, walking toward the front door.

"India! India!" Nancy yelled from the table.

"Yes, Mother!" India said, turning around.

"Make sure you open the club on time, 'cause we have a lot of money to make tonight!" Nancy said sarcastically.

India angrily shook her head and walked to the front door. After she got into her Range Rover, she sped off down the street with tears dripping down her face.

"I love the way you fuck me, Ricky!" Gloria yelled. Ricky had Gloria bent over the king-size bed with his long, hard dick deep inside her wet pussy. At the same time, he had a seven-inch distance-controlled vibrator inside her tight asshole. The small remote control was inside of his hand. A black leather neck choker was strapped around Gloria's neck. Ricky had the long leather strap wrapped around his wrist, pulling it every time he would stroke in and out of her throbbing pussy. Gloria was a cold freak! The rougher the sex, the better she like it. She had no boundaries when she would get with her secret black lover. Anal sex, oral, ass spankings, golden showers—was all a part of her sexual résumé.

"Oh my God, I'm having another orgasm!" Gloria shouted, feeling the double penetration moving inside her body. Ricky continued to stroke hard and deep, bringing Gloria total satisfaction.

"Ahhh! 'Mr. Orgasm!' I, I love this black dick!" she groaned in ecstasy. Her body was tingling all over with pleasure.

"I'm your bitch! Fuck this pussy! Fuck this white pussy!" Gloria grunted. Ricky stroked harder as he pulled on the leather neck strap. The remote control in his hand to the vibrator was turned on high. He could feel the vibration every time his dick slid inside her wet pussy. Gloria's neck was dark red. Her freshly manicured fingers gripped the silk sheets. Tears of pain and pleasure fell down from her blue eyes.

"Bitch, what's my name? Tell me, bitch!" Ricky shouted.

"'Mr. Orgasm!' Your name . . . is 'Mr. Orgasm!' Oh, oh, I'm coming again! Mr. Orgasm, oh, oh, oh!" Gloria shouted out slumping down on the bed. Ricky slid out his hard dick, but he left the vibrator still stuck inside her ass. He reached over and grabbed the small ass-paddle from the bed. After he wrapped the strap tighter around his hand, he said, "You've been a bad girl, and you know what happens to bad girls, don't you?"

"Yes, Daddy," Gloria said in a seductive voice.

Ricky raised his right hand high up in the air, and then came down with the wooden paddle hard on her round, white ass.

Smack, smack, smack!

"Yes, Daddy! Yes, Daddy! I've been a bad girl!" Gloria chanted as she started coming once again.

Chapter Twelve

Naughty & Nice

A few hours later

"Everything is ready for tonight, Nancy. I'll have my security team working out front and inside of the club," Big Nook said, sitting in the chair right across from her desk.

"Nook, I need you to put an extra guard inside the VIP section. Too many people be sneaking in there and messing with my celebrity clientele. You know how celebrities are. When they come out to enjoy themselves, they don't want to be hassled by nagging fans. The rapper Eve and a few of the Sixers' wives might stop by for the show tonight. I want them all to enjoy the show without being disturbed," Nancy said.

"I'll get right on it," Nook replied. "Anything else?"

Before Nancy could answer, there was a soft knock at the door. The timing was perfect, Big Nook thought to himself. He told one of his security workers to knock on the door five minutes after he had entered. Then once Nancy opened her office door, start feeding her a bogus story about seeing mice running around in the VIP section. The distraction gave Big Nook just enough time to place the mini tape recorder underneath her large desk.

"Damn mice!" Nancy said, very irritated. "Big Nook, I need you to call the exterminator."

"If there is a few of those little bastards running around, they'll all be dead before showtime," Big Nook promised, walking out of the office.

Nancy shut the door behind him and walked back over to her desk and sat down. After hearing another soft tap on the door, she said, "Who is it now?"

The doorknob turned, and Flex stuck his head inside. Nancy's frown turned into a big smile.

"Come in; lock the door," she said eagerly. Big Nook stood on the balcony and grinned. He looked down at India sitting at the table, typing something on her laptop computer. He looked at the few dancers that had come to work early to practice their show routines. Fifteen minutes later, he saw Flex walk out of Nancy's office with a satisfied look on his face. The dancers were still practicing. India was deep into her laptop computer. After Big Nook got off his cell phone with Detective Hightower, he thought about the hidden tape recorder and just smiled and shook his head.

After three hours of hard, rough, sex, Gloria and Ricky were laid out on the huge king-size bed. The rich, older, white female cuddled up under her young black lover. As their two naked bodies held each other, the soulful voice of Marvin Gaye flowed from the speakers. Ricky fucked Gloria every way she wanted it done. Her sore body had so many orgasms that she lost count after the seventh one. As soon as Marvin's soulful voice started to fade away, the melodic voice of Anita Baker quickly replaced it. Gloria sat up on her elbow and looked into Ricky's eyes.

"Promise me something," she said earnestly.

"It depends on what it is," Ricky said, looking in her serious blue eyes.

"I want you to promise me that you'll always be honest with me."

"I'll always be honest with you, Gloria," Ricky said seriously.

"We both know that out little secret affair won't last forever. We are two people from two different worlds," she said.

"Where is all of this coming from?"

"The heart! I could never have you the way that I would like. I've already dropped my shield for you, Ricky. That's something I never did for my own husband. You are a very handsome young, black man, and I'm an older white woman still trying to hold on to my youth."

"So what are you saying?" he asked, seeing the tears well up in her eyes.

"I'm saying that when you're finally ready to move on, just don't leave me in the dark. At least give me the opportunity to save my old heart," Gloria said, as the tears started falling down her face.

"Gloria—"

"Just tell me you'll do it," she said, cutting him off.

Ricky stared deep into her watery, ocean-blue eyes and said, "I promise you that I will always be 100 percent honest with you. If I ever feel as though it's time for me to move on with my life, I will look you into those beautiful blue eyes and tell you it's over," he said softly.

After they lay and rested for a few more moments, they took a warm shower together, and both got dressed. Gloria had to get back to her suburban Philadelphia mansion, and Ricky had to hurry and pick up his daughter Asia at school. When they walked out the front door, Ricky walked Gloria over to her Rolls-Royce Phantom and watched as she got inside. She put on her designer frames and rolled down the window.

"I'll see you when time permits," she said with a smile.

"Before you leave, can I ask you just one question?" Ricky said. "And be honest."

"Sure, go ahead."

"Can you tell me what it is that you are so afraid of?" he asked seriously.

Gloria smiled as she took off her frames. With a sigh, she said, "I'm afraid of loving someone who cannot love me back."

Ricky stood there in silence as Gloria put her frames back on, smiled, and rolled up the window. Then he watched as she slowly pulled off inside her quarter-million dollar automobile and disappeared. Once she was gone, Ricky got into his BMW and sped off. He couldn't wait to see her beautiful smiling face again.

After Ricky picked up Asia from school, he took her back home and helped her with her homework. Once they finished, they played a few games of jacks and watched cartoons together. Before Ricky left, Asia asked him about India again. He promised her that she would see India soon. There are always things that you want to protect a child from, and heartbreak is one of them. His goal was never to have his daughter long for anything or anyone. This was one of the reasons he opted never to bring his daughter around any women because children become easily attached.

On his way to the club, Ricky picked up DJ Twist. When they pulled up, they immediately noticed Roscoe's big black Escalade was parked out front. Roscoe, Damon, and Flex were all standing outside of it talking and laughing as if they didn't have a care in the world. Ricky despised Roscoe so he hoped that he wouldn't say anything out of line.

"Here comes the fake-ass lover boy," Roscoe said, as soon as Ricky and DJ Twist walked by. Damon and Flex both started laughing.

"'Mr. Orgasm!' How fucking gay is that?" Roscoe laughed.

Ricky passed Twist his sports bag and walked up to Roscoe. "Do you have a problem with me, Roscoe?" Ricky said angrily. "If so, then we can handle it like two grown men." Roscoe didn't even blink; he just lifted his white T-shirt up, letting Ricky see the Desert Eagle handgun tucked inside his jeans.

"Lover boy . . . 'Mr. Orgasm,' or whatever they call you now, you're way out of your league, partna!"

Ricky stood there with rage in his eyes. He thought about Asia and started slowly backing away.

"This ain't the old days, Roscoe. I ain't scared no more! Ain't nobody chasing me home now," Ricky said.

"You will *always* be the scared little punk that we chased home. Ricky, ain't nothing changed but your gay-ass name!" Roscoe spat as Damon and Flex busted out laughing.

"Is there a problem, Ricky?" His friend Thunder said, walking out of the club.

"There will be, big boy, if you don't hurry up and get him," Roscoe said.

"Come on, Ricky, it ain't worth it," Thunder said, grabbing Ricky by the shoulder and walking him inside the club. After Twist followed Ricky and Thunder into the club, Roscoe, Damon, and Flex all started laughing.

"Fuck that soft-ass, panty-wearing motherfucker! He's lucky I ain't put a cap in his bitch ass!"

"Why didn't you?" Damon asked.

"Because my girl will probably be mad at me for killing her favorite exotic dancer," he said laughing. "Flex, I'll see you later. Keep up the good work. And keep an eye on that cop, Big Nook," Roscoe said as he and Damon got back into the truck.

"Don't worry, Roscoe, I got you," Flex said, walking back into the club.

"Light that blunt up. That bitch-ass nigga got my blood pressure up!" Roscoe said, starting up his Escalade and driving off.

Back inside the club, Thunder and Ricky stood by the stage talking.

"Don't let that stupid-ass nigga fuck up your mood, Ricky. That's all Flex wants to do. It's Wednesday. Tonight, we'll have a full house cheering us on. Those troublemakers ain't worth it. You bigger than that; don't feed into their little trap," Thunder said, putting his arm around Ricky's shoulder.

"Thunder, I'm really tired of that nigga Roscoe! That nigga think he's so tough, and mothering or no one can touch him. The only reason I ain't beat the shit out of his bitch ass was because he had a gun on him. I have a little daughter to worry about," Ricky said.

"Just don't feed into his bullshit game. A man like him you have to find his weakness first, *then* you attack him," Thunder said.

"What if he ain't got no weakness?" Ricky asked.

"Ricky, *everybody* has a weakness. Some people's weakness is their money, while others are love or their children. We all have weaknesses," Thunder said walking away and leaving Ricky alone to gather his thoughts. When Ricky looked up, he noticed India sitting at the table staring at him. He grabbed his bag and walked over to her.

"What's up, pretty?" he said.

"You!" India replied.

"What about me?" Ricky asked seeing the serious expression on her face.

"Ricky . . . Ricky . . ."

"What, India? Say it," he said anxiously.

India just sadly shook her head. Her mouth wouldn't let her say what her heart had told her to speak. She turned around her laptop computer and said, "We have a winner for your ultimate fan contest."

"Is *that* it? There's *nothing* else you want to tell me?" Ricky asked, relieved.

After a long sigh, she said, "No, Ricky, that's it. Next Friday, the club will pay for you and your lucky female fan to have an all-expenses-paid dinner to any restaurant you choose in the city."

"Is that all?" Ricky asked again.

"Yes, that's all I had to tell you," India lied.

"Well, you can hook everything up; you can even pick the restaurant. Tell the winner I'm looking forward to meeting her. You know the game, India. It's all about our fans," Ricky said, turning around, and walking away in disappointment.

India sat there at the table with a confused look on her face and sadness boiling inside her soul.

"India! Hey, India!" Ricky yelled back.

"Yeah, Ricky," she turned and said.

"I forgot to tell you that Asia asked about you again."

Before India could respond, Ricky disappeared behind the large curtain. She really had a soft spot for his daughter. She wasn't happy about the way things had gone. Her heart and mind were so conflicted. It's always hard to shake feelings when you know what you want but see many obstacles in your way. India turned back around and looked at her laptop computer screen. The winner of Ricky's ultimate fan contest was a woman named Tammy Mathis. She was a thirty-year-old female who lived in North Philly. It was India's job to notify the contest winner and tell her what she had won. She reached into her jacket pocket and took out her cell phone. She had the entire woman's info on the screen in front of her. Then she turned around and saw Ricky practicing his moves on stage. After dialing the woman's phone number, she waited.

"Hello," A woman's voice answered. "Hello . . . Hello—"

Without saying a word, India ended the call.

Chapter Thirteen

The Freaks Come Out at Night

Club Chances, Wednesday night, 8:30 p.m.

A long line of excited women were all waiting to get inside of the club. Beautiful females dressed in their most expensive, newest fashions, smelling and looking their best. The ballers and hustlers were all hanging around showing off their most expensive cars with twenty-two-inch rims and banging systems. So many blunts were lit that the strong smell of marijuana filled the air.

A white Mercedes stretch limo pulled up in front of the club. Big Nook and two of his men quickly cleared out the path. When the chauffeur walked around and opened the door, four beautiful women all exited the limousine. Two were black, two white. Three of them were the wives of NBA players. The other was the fiancée of a professional football player.

Big Nook quickly escorted the four lovely women up to the private VIP section. Already in the VIP section were some of Philly's top female celebrities. Some of the celebrities were Jill Scott, Patti LaBelle, Eve, Charli Baltimore, Vivian Green, and the singing duo Floetry, to name just a few. Lil' Kim and a few of her New York girlfriends were also inside the VIP, and all were enjoying themselves. The club was packed with women. There were women of all races who had just come out to have a good time. Women were sipping on margaritas and daiquiris. They bought bottles of Moët, Cristal, and Hpnotiq. A few women were already tipsy, shouting out their favorite dancers' names.

Nancy was standing all alone on the balcony. Every time another woman walked through her doors, she saw dollar signs. India was standing in the back of the club lost in thought. Working at the club with her mother was no longer fun. It was now a job that India had regretted taking. The only reason she stuck around and didn't quit was because of Ricky. Seeing Ricky coming and going was worth all the bullshit her mother would take her through, she thought.

DJ Twist was mixing and scratching on the turntables. The bass from the songs was banging hard out of the speakers. The women were laughing and conversing while waiting for the show to start. Ricky was standing behind the stage curtain, looking through the peephole. He looked up and saw Nancy on the balcony. Even as he stood behind the curtain, he could see the look of greed on her face. As he continued to scan the large crowd of women, he spotted India standing by herself on the back wall. Out of all the women inside the club, to him, India was the prettiest one there. The only one he wanted, but because of certain circumstances, he couldn't have her. He was once her mother's young, secret lover, and for that reason, Ricky decided to keep his distance from India.

"Hey, what's up, Ricky? You ready to do your thing?" Thunder asked, standing beside him.

"Yeah, I'ma little nervous, but I'm ready," Ricky said stretching his arms over his head. Another exotic dancer walked up and joined in their conversation.

"Packed house today, huh, fellas?" Neo said.

"There's more people here than it was on Monday night," Thunder said, adjusting his bow tie.

"Ricky, you all right? I heard about the little incident with Roscoe earlier," Neo said in a concerned voice.

"Yeah, I'm fine, Neo. That punk doesn't scare me," he said.

"Do you see that pretty redbone over there? The one standing by the tall, brown-skinned chick?" Neo said, pointing his finger out the hole in the curtain.

"Yeah, she's pretty. Who is she?" Ricky asked.

"That's Roscoe's fiancée. He drops her off at the club every Monday and Wednesday," Neo said.

"Is that right?" Ricky said with a conniving smile.

"Just thought I'd let you know," Neo said nonchalantly, walking away.

"So what do you think, Thunder?" Ricky asked.

"I don't think you need to ask me, Ricky. Like I told you earlier, *everybody* has a weakness," Thunder said with a smile. "Everybody."

Once again, all the lights in the club went out. All except the fluorescent green lights that lit up the large stage. The women started screaming, clapping, whistling, and yelling. Then, a few colorful ceiling lights started blinking on and off. Women were running up to the front of the stage trying to get a better view. A few women stood up on their chairs.

"Are y'all ladies ready to get this party started?" DJ Twist shouted out in the microphone. A loud roar of female voices instantly filled the club.

"Are y'all beautiful women out there ready to be entertained by twenty of the best exotic dancers on the whole East Coast?" DJ Twist yelled into the mic. Women started screaming at the top of their lungs. After DJ Twist released his hand off the record, the crowd went crazy. Whodini's classic rap song, "The Freaks Come out at Night" started banging out of the speakers. While the women cheered and sang along to the classic chorus, the large curtain started slowing opening.

After the stage curtain had been pulled back, twenty well-toned, greased down bodies stood on the large stage. The twenty men all performed a well-choreographed dance. Each exotic dancer was dressed in a pair of black male thongs and a black bow tie. After their breathtaking performance had ended, the stage curtain started to close, and all the dancers walked backstage.

One at a time, each of the exotic dancers performed their solo routine. After Thunder did his thing, Neo performed right behind him. The last two exotic performers that were left to dance were Flex and Ricky. Flex was determined to outperform Ricky. Even though he had only five minutes to do his thing on stage, Flex had a few tricks up his sleeve. He walked out on stage to Nelly's classic song "Hot in Herre." Flex was dressed in a fireman's outfit; a fire hat, jacket, and pants. The women went wild and crazy as he strolled across the stage and jumped on the dance pole. Flex threw his jacket and hat into the screaming crowd. Women were pushing and shoving each other to grab the items. The women who stood on the balcony were throwing bills all in the air. The club was raining with money.

After Flex slid down his pants, he ran out into the boisterous crowd. Big Nook and his staff had to pull the screaming women from off him. One of the women had managed to snatch off his thong. Without a care in the world, Flex leaped on top of a table and started grooving to the music. The women were getting the show of their lives. Even India stood back, impressed by Flex's erotic performance.

When Flex had finally made it backstage, even some of the other dancers had to congratulate him on a job well done. Nancy had watched it all from the balcony. And she couldn't wait to meet her young lover Flex back at the hotel that she had waiting for them after the club closed. Her pussy was already wet with anticipation. Once again, the lights all went out.

"Y'all know what time it is!" DJ Twist shouted. "Ladies, stand up; get out y'all seats! Put the bottles of Cristal and Belvedere down and let's welcome to the stage the one and only exotic male stripper on the planet—'Mr. Orgasm!'" DJ Twist shouted in the microphone.

"We want our Orgasm! We want our Orgasm! We want our Orgasm!" women kept yelling. When DJ Twist let his hand off the record, 50 Cent and Lil' Kim's classic song, "Magic Stick," banged hard out of the speakers. The women went crazy.

When the stage curtain was pulled back, 'Mr. Orgasm' was standing on the stage with an entire pimp outfit on. He was wearing a big black mink hat with a matching mink coat. Black shades covered his eyes, and about ten gold chains were hanging around his neck. In one of his hands, he had a long, shiny cane. In the other, he had a large signature pimp cup.

'Mr. Orgasm' strolled across the stage like he owned it. After he laid down his cane and cup, he tossed his hat and chains into the cheering crowd. A fight broke out between two of the women. Big Nook and his crew quickly separated the two females and escorted them both out of the club. 'Mr. Orgasm' slid down the mink coat and stepped out of it. The mink coat was a gift from Gloria; he wasn't tossing that in the crowd.

After he stepped out of his coat, he ran and did a line of backflips across the stage. When he finished, he landed in a perfect leg split. Once again, the women went wild. 'Mr. Orgasm' flowed to the rhythm of the beat. His beautiful body made love to the stage like it was his woman. Just like on Flex's performance, the bills filled the air, and the money rained down all over the club. In the middle of his erotic performance, DJ Twist mixed in another classic song. The song was called "Get Your Freak On" by Missy Elliot.

Before "Mr. Orgasm" had ended his breathtaking performance, he grabbed his two dozen red roses and started tossing them out into the crowd. The women were pushing and shoving one another to get one. The last rose he held in his hand was the yellow one. He walked along the stage searching for the special female he would give it to. Women were yelling his name, begging for the rose to be given to them. India stood in the back with a sad look on her face. This was the part of Ricky's performance that she hated the most. "Mr. Orgasm" jumped off the stage into the arms of all his screaming female fans. The women grabbed and pulled on his arms and legs like he was a rock star.

He walked up to the chosen female. She was a short, attractive redbone. Her excited girlfriend stood by her side. He leaned over and whispered something in her ear. Then smiling, she nodded her head and accepted his yellow rose. Ricky danced his way back through the crowd of swarming women. The other exotic dancers were spread out all over the club. Some were giving lap dances, while others were standing around grinding on horny females. Flex was bragging to two women about his performance. Thunder had an attractive dark-skinned female scooped up in his huge arms. Neo was giving a white woman a lap dance. DJ Twist was mixing and scratching on the turntables. Nancy was already inside of her private office, counting money that the club had made from the door. Big Nook and his men kept the crowd calm and in order. Artie, the bartender, was filling up drinks left and right. It was like one big after party; 300 women and twenty handsome, exotic, male strippers. Panties were wet, dicks were hard, asses bounced, and the music was banging loud and hard.

India watched as the lucky female with the yellow rose eased her way through the crowd. Her girlfriend pushed her on. Ricky saw the lust in her eyes. When he opened the door and went inside, she followed, then she locked it from the inside. India wiped the lone tear from her face before anyone noticed. When the coast was clear, she eased out the door of the club and got into her truck. With Ricky on her mind, the tears started falling once again.

Chapter Fourteen

Guilty Pleasures

"So you said your name was Tori, right?" Ricky asked looking straight into her lustful brown eyes.

"Yeah," Tori responded standing against the wall with her hands behind her back. Before Tori came to meet Ricky inside the room, she gave her friend Malinda her 3-carat engagement ring to hold for her. Tori stood at five foot four and weighed 135 pounds. She had an expensive weave that hung down to the center of her back. Her gorgeous body was just as tight as her weave; her hourglass measurements were 36-25-38.

"We only have half an hour. Tell me, beautiful, what would you like to do?" Ricky asked moving slowly toward her.

"Whatever you like, just as long as you use a condom," Tori said with a serious smile. Ricky opened up his hand and showed Tori the Magnum condom inside.

"I'm always prepared," he said, pulling her into his arms and grinding his body up against her. Ricky started kissing all around Tori's sensitive neck. Each time his lips made contact, they sent chills up and down her spine. She reached her arms around him and cupped his ass. Ricky put his hand under her dress and ripped off her soaking wet thong. Tori was so turned on that she didn't resist. With two fingers, he started playing with her pussy.

"Ohhh!" Tori moaned, as she enjoyed the two-finger clit massage Ricky was giving her. Ricky pulled back and just stared at her. He could see in her eyes that she was burning with desire.

"Take off your dress!" he ordered. Tori slid the dress down her body and stepped out of it. Then, without Ricky asking her, she took off her bra also. Ricky slid down his thong and kicked it to the side. Tori's eyes almost popped out of her head when she saw Ricky's majestic dick at full erection.

"Damn! You hung like a horse!" she said nervously yet excited.

"Yeah, I hope you enjoy riding one," he said, grabbing her hand and walking her over to the small cushioned bench. Ricky sat down and opened up the Magnum condom.

"I'll put it on," Tori said, taking it from his hand. She grabbed his hard dick and slid the large condom all the way down. It was a perfect fit. He grabbed Tori and easily lifted her naked body on to his. Tori wrapped her arms around his shoulders and held on. Slowly, Ricky slid his hard dick inside of her wet pussy.

"Ohh! God!" she moaned. Holding on to her waist, Ricky slid in and out of her. Then he went inside of her as deep as he could go.

"Oh, I . . . I feel it in my stomach!" Tori grunted. Ricky kept it there and started circling his hips. "Ohhh! Ahhh! That's my spot! I'm coming!" Tori yelled out in pleasure. Ricky stood up from the bench with her wrapped inside his strong arms. He started carrying her around the room, with his hard dick still inside her. Tori came two more times.

"Ahhh! My God!" she screamed as tears of pleasure fell from her eyes. Ricky laid her down on the soft, carpeted floor. Her body was trembling with pleasure. It had only been ten minutes, and she had already come three times.

He climbed on top of Tori's trembling body and placed her legs on his broad shoulders.

"Please go slow!" Tori begged.

Ricky smiled and said, "Don't worry, beautiful, I will." Then he slowly slid his dick back inside of her wetness. Ricky pinned her body down and started delivering long, slow strokes.

"Ohh! Yes! God!" Tori moaned out. Each time Ricky went inside of her, he would go in as far as he could. Then he moved his hips around like a professional belly dancer. Left, right, up and down. Tori came two more times.

"Ahhh! I . . . I . . . com . . . com . . . coming!" She screamed.

Ricky put his lips to her ear and whispered, "Beautiful, this is just the beginning."

Tori couldn't believe that she had come so much in such a short period of time. Her fiancé Roscoe had never made her come more than twice. Ricky was still rock hard, taking his precious time, stroking slow. He turned Tori around on all fours. Then he held onto her hips and started fucking her in the doggie-style position. This time, he stroked harder and faster.

"Ahhh! Yes! Yes! Ohh! 'Mr. Orgasm!' I feel you all up inside of me!" Tori moaned. "Ohh!"

Ricky kept stroking. While he stroked, he slapped her phat ass.

"Oh shit! I'm having another orgasm!" Tori yelled out.

"Ahhh! Ohhh!" she moaned as the powerful orgasm swept throughout her body. When Ricky pulled out of her, Tori's naked body slumped down to the floor. In the doggie-style position, Ricky had fucked her hard and aggressive. He showed her pussy no mercy. Ricky looked down at Tori, as she was now lying in the fetal position. Her entire body was still trembling with pleasure. He walked over and kneeled down in front of her.

"Beautiful, I really enjoyed myself. Thank you," he said softly. Tori didn't even respond. Her half hour with Ricky was the best sex that she had ever had in her life, and it was the first time Tori ever had an orgasm from penetration alone. Ricky kissed her on the forehead, then stood up before walking over to the towel rack. He grabbed a dry towel and walked back over to Tori. Her body was still trembling. He took the towel and wiped the wetness from around her inner thighs, pussy, and legs. This was something totally new to her. Whenever she and Roscoe had finished sex, he would immediately roll over and fall asleep, never paying attention to her needs, only his own. After they both dressed, Ricky gave Tori his business card.

"Call me, and the next time, I promise you, beautiful, that it will be ten times better," he said. "Can I keep these?" Ricky asked holding her thong in his hand.

"Yeah, go head," Tori said dreamily.

Ricky put the thong inside his sports bag. After he zipped his bag up, he walked over and kissed Tori on her forehead again.

"Hope to see you soon," he said before walking out of the room.

Five minutes later, Tori walked out of the room, more content than ever. She saw Ricky talking to Nancy, but she kept walking on. The music was banging, and everybody was still enjoying themselves. No one seemed to pay her any mind. Her girlfriend Malinda saw her and quickly ran up to her. Malinda saw the satisfied look in her eyes and said, "Damn! That good, huh?"

"Where's Flex? Did he see me?" Tori asked nervously.

"No, that nigga is too busy running around bragging and chasing pussy," Malinda said. She grabbed Tori's hand and pulled her into a secluded area of the club.

"What happened?" she asked curiously. Tori looked into her best friend's eyes and said softly, "Malinda, that man just fucked the shit out of me in that room! I came about five times!" Tori said seriously.

"What? But y'all was only up there for half an hour," Malinda said, shocked.

"I'm telling you, Malinda, 'Mr. Orgasm' just fucked my brains out, girl. My pussy is still hurting. The nigga's dick is way bigger than Roscoe's."

"What? Oh my God!" Malinda laughed.

"After we finished, he said thank you, and then wiped me down with a towel," Tori said, shaking her head in total disbelief.

"I don't think he even came because his dick was still hard when he pulled out of me."

"Damn! I told you, girl! I told you about the rumors!" Malinda said.

"He took my panties as a souvenir.

"Girl, you crazy!" Malinda laughed. "You gonna see him again?"

"I hope so. He told me the next time it will be ten times better."

Malinda just stood there shaking her head. After hearing all the details, her panties were filled with wetness. She gave Tori back her engagement ring and said, "So now, what's up with you and Roscoe?"

"I don't know, but soon we gonna have to sit down and have a nice long talk," Tori said.

"You're gonna tell him?" Malinda asked, shocked.

"Hell no! But I *am* gonna tell Roscoe that we need to slow down with our marriage plans. Right now, Malinda, I have a lot of things to think about," Tori said seriously.

"I told you, girl, that his sex be turning women out! I told you!" Malinda said.

"I'm cool," Tori said softly—but unconvincingly.

"No, the hell you ain't. Your body is still trembling," Malinda reminded her.

After leaving the club, Tori and Malinda saw Roscoe's big black truck and walked across the street and got inside.

"Enjoy yourself?" Roscoe asked, pulling off down the street.

"Yeah, I had a nice time," Tori said.

"Good. I'm hungry. Let's go to Denny's," Roscoe said. "You hungry?"

"I'm starving!" Tori replied.

Malinda sat back on the backseat and didn't say a word. While Roscoe and Damon were talking, Tori looked back and shook her head. After Malinda winked, Tori turned back around. On the drive to Denny's, her satisfied body never stopped trembling.

Chapter Fifteen

Keep It on the Down Low

Inside the men's bathroom, Ricky, Neo, and Thunder were all talking.

"Ricky, I saw her face when she left the club. What did you do to that girl?" Neo asked.

"I did what I do," he said.

"You must have done one hell of a job!" Thunder added, patting him on the back.

"Yeah, but y'all know what?" Ricky said seriously.

"What's that?" the two said in unison.

"I can tell she's a nice girl. She was just infatuated and curious, just like most of those women are. So I'm not gonna hurt her, because my beef ain't with her; it's with her man," Ricky said.

"Do you think she's happy with him?" Neo asked.

"Probably not sexually; maybe not at all. One thing that I know for sure is, when a woman is totally satisfied with her man, she will not let nobody enter their love circle. It don't matter how handsome, rich, or how nice the person's body is. A real woman will not violate herself or the man she loves," Ricky said.

"Well, where the hell are the real women at?" Thunder asked. "My cousin went to prison, and his wife left him after just seven months in. His own *wife!*"

"Yeah, and look at all the wives that come here to get their freak on. All the wives who running around creeping on the down low. All the wives we fucking, then sending them back home with lustful memories and wet pussies," Neo added.

"All I know, fellas, is we all have a soul mate out there somewhere. One thing for sure is, I won't settle for anyone that's less than a queen. I won't stop doing my thing until I'm 100 percent positive that I've found my soul mate," Ricky said seriously. He looked into the mirror and checked his appearance. After wiping his goatee, he and his friends walked out of the bathroom.

After the show had ended and all the women had left the club, India stood back waiting as the club workers cleaned up the club. Nancy and Big Nook were inside her office with the door locked. Most of the dancers had gotten dressed and left. DJ Twist had packed up his equipment and left the club when his girlfriend showed up, beeping the horn outside. India watched as Ricky and Thunder was walking toward her.

"Hey, India, see you next Monday," Thunder said.

"All right, Thunder," she replied with a mile. "Nice show you did, Ricky."

"Thank you, India. Where were you? I didn't see you."

"I was chilling in the back. You know me. I like to stay out of the way," she said.

"Did you get with the contest winner?" he asked.

"Yeah, everything is set. I'll call your cell phone and give you the details tomorrow. If you don't answer, I'll leave a message on your voice mail service. It will be definitely next Friday."

"That's fine; I'll make sure I'm free."

"Ricky, Ricky—"

"Yes, India, what is it?"

After a long sigh, she said, "I just wanted to tell you again how much I really enjoyed your show."

"What about me?" Thunder asked jokingly.

"You too, Thunder," she said playfully.

India walked over to the door and stood in the doorway. She watched as Ricky and Thunder both got in their cars. Thunder quickly pulled off down the street inside his blue Ford Excursion. Ricky pulled his car up in front of the club. The window slowly rolled down.

"India, can I ask you something?"

She walked over to the car and said, "Yes, what is it, Ricky?"

Ricky looked into her beautiful face. "India, do you believe that everyone has a soul mate?"

"Yes, I do, Ricky. God wouldn't have it any other way," she said with a smile.

"Thank you, India," he said, winking his eye and pulling off.

After the club had been cleaned by the workers, India left and drove home.

A few hours later,
inside the Sheraton Hotel by the airport

"Yes! Baby! Oh yes! Fuck me harder, Flex! Fuck me harder, Flex! Yes! Oh yes!" Nancy yelled out. Flex had Nancy bent over the bed, fucking her from behind. Before they had started, she made Flex take a fifty milligram Viagra. Sweat covered both of their naked bodies. Nancy was so loud that the couple inside the room next door could hear every word she said. Flex was fucking Nancy all over the room.

Nancy was enjoying every bit of it. She had manipulated her young lover to kill her husband so that she could collect the insurance money after he died. After twenty-three years of marriage, Nancy was tired of the same old thing. She wanted a new life; one with more excitement. Even when her husband was alive, Nancy was having a secret affair with Ricky. Ricky knew it was wrong, so he decided to terminate the affair. Nancy was very upset with Ricky, but it didn't take her long to find his sexual replacement: Flex. After Nancy had set up the whole plot, she paid Flex $20,000 to kill her husband. The police had interviewed everyone at the club, but they found no suspects, prints, or witnesses to help in the case.

"Oh! Fuck me harder! Fuck me harder, Flex!" Nancy yelled out. "Baby, I love this dick! Fuck me harder!" she screamed out, having another intense orgasm.

Outside in the hotel parking lot, Hightower was waiting inside his car. Big Nook had just left after giving him the cassette from the minitape recorder. Hightower was determined to get all the information he could get on Nancy and Flex.

He knew their every move. Secret trips to Atlantic City, private suites at expensive hotels, and even a surveillance tape of them having sex in a downtown hotel. Still, he knew he needed something more concrete and incriminating to get a grand jury indictment. He needed Nancy or Flex to say something about the murder on tape. Nothing was more incriminating than a suspect's own words. But Nancy's own actions had also been in Hightower's favor.

How can a woman work in the same office that her husband was murdered in? Hightower thought. Even a blind man could see that something wasn't right with that. Hightower was no fool.

After he waited another half hour, he pulled off and drove home.

***

Inside her bedroom, India's naked body was lying on top of the thick blanket. As the scented candles filled the calm air, she had her Jack Rabbit vibrator exploring her wetness. With Ricky on her mind and in her heart, India felt the powerful orgasms travel all throughout her naked body. After taking a quick shower, she got back in bed, hugged her pillow, and fell asleep with a smile on her face.

Chapter Sixteen

Who's That Lady?

Thursday morning

After Ricky snapped on Asia's safety belt and Nicole got in the backseat of his BMW, he slowly pulled off down the street. The car that Ricky had bought Nicole was currently in the repair shop, so Ricky decided to drop Asia off at her elementary school, and then take Nicole to her college.

"Daddy, can I go out with Ms. India again?" Asia pleaded.

"Sweetie, I'ma call Ms. India later and ask her if she would like to come take you out on Saturday," Ricky said while driving down Fifty-fourth Street. Nicole was sitting in the backseat talking on her cell phone.

"Sweetie, why do you like Ms. India so much?" Ricky asked curiously.

"Because she's nice, and she treats me nice too. Ms. India is pretty too," Asia said with smile. "Daddy, do you like Ms. India?"

"Yes, I like her. She's my friend."

"Is she your girlfriend?" Asia asked grinning.

"No, sweetie, me and Ms. India are just friends. Daddy doesn't have a girlfriend right now," Ricky said, amused.

"When you get a girlfriend, Daddy, can it be Ms. India?" Asia asked with a serious expression on her face.

"Ms. India might have a boyfriend already," he responded, laughing.

"She doesn't," Asia said with assurance.

"How do you know?" he asked, making a right turn down Fifty-first Street.

"Because she told me she didn't have a boyfriend when she took me to the zoo. She told me she's waiting for a nice man to be her boyfriend," Asia revealed.

"Oh, she did?"

"Yup. I mean yes. When I told Ms. India that you were a nice man, she just smiled."

"So you really like Ms. India, huh?" he asked, pulling his car up in front of Asia's school.

After Ricky unbuckled Asia's seat belt, he leaned over and kissed her on the cheek. "I'll ask Ms. India if she would like to take you out again. Be good, and I'll see you when school let's out."

"Okay, Daddy. I love you."

"I love you too, sweetie," he replied as he watched her get out of the car and shut the door. Nicole closed her cell phone, got out of the backseat, then climbed in the front passenger seat. Asia stood there with her teacher waving good-bye. After Ricky and Nicole waved good-bye, he slowly pulled down the street.

"I just got off the phone with Mrs. Langston," Nicole said excitedly.

"Who?"

"Mrs. Langston, my teacher that I told you about. The one who really wants to meet you."

"You have your teacher's phone number?" Ricky asked, curious.

"Yeah, she gave it to me after I told her that you were my brother," Nicole grinned.

"Girl, what is you up to now?"

"I'm just trying to hook you up," Nicole said with a smile.

"I don't need no hooking up. So stop lying and tell me the truth," Ricky said seriously.

"Okay. I'm having some problems with psychology, and I figured—"

"That you can introduce your teacher to meet me, your exotic dancer older brother, and she would cut you some slack," he said, cutting her off.

"Yeah, something like that," Nicole calmly said.

"I don't know about this, Nicole. I have too many female friends now. I need to get rid of some of them," he said, driving down Spring Garden Street.

"Please, Ricky . . . Please, you'll like her, and she's real pretty," Nicole begged.

Ricky just smiled and shook his head. "Girl, you're something else!" he laughed.

When Nancy walked through the front door, India was sitting on the sofa typing into her laptop computer. She watched as her mother hung up her coat, then sat down in the empty love seat.

"Next time, can you at least call and tell me that you're gonna be out all night?" India said.

"Girl, don't worry about me. I'll be fine. Did you call the bank this morning?" she asked, kicking off her shoes and putting her feet on the coffee table.

"Yes, Mom, I called the bank. All the checks have cleared, all the money was deposited, and they want to give you a new American Express, etc.," India said.

After picking up her shoes, Nancy walked over to the stairs. "I'm tired. I'm taking myself a hot shower, and then a nice long nap. If anybody calls me, tell 'em I'm asleep and take a message," she instructed while walking up the stairs. India didn't even respond. She just turned her head in disappointment and went back to typing on her computer.

Tori was standing in the doorway of the apartment, watching Roscoe get inside his Escalade and quickly pulling off down the street. After he left, she shut the door and ran over to the sofa. She grabbed her cell phone off the coffee table and quickly dialed "Mr. Orgasm's" cell phone number. The voice mail recording instantly came on.

"I'm sorry that I'm unable to get your call, but please leave me a message and I promise to get back with you ASAP."

"Hello. 'Mr. Orgasm.' It's me, Tori, the girl from the club last night. I really enjoyed myself with you and would really like to see you again . . . soon. You can call me back on my girlfriend's number I gave you. I thought about you all night long! Anyway, I'm free whenever you are. Hope you call. Bye." She closed her cell phone, sat back on the sofa, and smiled. After her half-hour sex session with "Mr. Orgasm," she couldn't get him off her mind. While Roscoe lay snoring all night long, Tori was in bed staring up at the ceiling, thinking of all those wonderful orgasms, which had given her body the chills. When Tori heard the knock at the front door, she snapped out of her lustful daydream and ran over and opened it. Malinda walked inside the apartment and just stared at her. After looking into Tori's glowing eyes, Malinda just shook her head.

"Damn, girl, look at you. I ain't seen you glow this much since Roscoe gave you that diamond ring! Damn! That dick must be voodoo, 'cause he damn sure put a spell on you! I warned you about that nigga," Malinda said. "Now that dick got you feening like a crackhead!"

On the corner of Seventeenth and Spring Garden street

Ricky pulled up in front of the Community College of Philadelphia and found an empty parking space. The street was full of students and teachers, all rushing to get to their morning classes. He looked out the window and noticed an attractive white woman standing in front of the large steps.

"Who's that?" Ricky asked as he pointed. Nicole looked at her brother and with a smile, said, "That's Mrs. Langston."

"Damn! She's fine!"

"I told you she was pretty."

"What is she? She looks Spanish."

"She's Italian," Nicole said getting out of the car. Ricky got out of the car as well and followed behind Nicole. The woman saw them both walking toward her.

"Hey, Mrs. Langston, this is my brother, Ricky," Nicole said with a big smile.

"How are you?" the woman asked, shaking Ricky's hand.

"I'm late for my first class. I'll see you later, Ricky, and I'll see you in class, Mrs. Langston," Nicole said rushing off.

Ricky stared into the beautiful woman's green eyes.

"So what do you like to be called?" he asked politely.

"Oh, I'm sorry. My name is Victoria," she said, blushing.

"My sister told me that you're Italian. Langston doesn't sound Italian to me."

"That's my husband's last name. My maiden name is Victoria Marcello."

"Husband?"

"Yeah. Do you have a problem with that?" Victoria asked seriously.

"Not if you don't."

"I came to one of your shows a few weeks ago, and I must say that I was *very* impressed with the way you dance," Victoria said.

"Thank you," Ricky said smiling, eyeing her from head to toe.

Victoria stood at five foot six and had long, silky black hair, green eyes, and a nice, petite body. Her pretty teeth were as white as snow, and her face was drop-dead gorgeous. She was a thirty-eight-year-old psychology professor, who had been working at the college for four years.

"Nicole said that you wanted to meet me."

"Yes, I did. Like I said, I was very impressed with the way you dance. When I found out that Nicole was your younger sister, I told her that I would really like to meet you," she said flashing a beautiful smile.

"Lucky me."

"It can be," she smiled. "So tell me, where did you get the name 'Mr. Orgasm'?" she said flirtatiously.

"I earned it," he flirted back.

"Is that so?" Victoria blushed.

"Yes. And I do my very best to live up to my reputation," Ricky said seriously. Victoria looked him up and down, liking everything she saw and heard.

"Are you busy this Saturday, 'Mr. Orgasm'?"

"Not if you're in need of my services."

"I see you are a very confident man."

"Very," Ricky said, licking his lips. Victoria went into her purse and took out a small piece of paper.

"This is my number and address. Call me."

Ricky took it, and then passed her his business card. "I'm sure you know, beautiful, that nothing in this world is free," he expressed.

Victoria looked into his serious eyes and smiled. “That’s just the way I like it. I’ll call you tonight, and we can discuss all the details,” she said, swishing away.

Chapter Seventeen

Lustful Eyes

Later that morning,
Tasker Home Projects, South Philly

"Roscoe, I'ma get your money!" the man cried out.

"Nigga, you been saying that for a whole week. Fuck, you think I'ma sucka?" Roscoe yelled, pointing his .45 at the scared man's head.

"Kill this motherfucker!" Damon yelled.

"*Please,* man! Please," the man cried.

The man's terrified girlfriend sat on the couch crying. Their one-year-old son was asleep inside his crib in the bedroom.

"Please, man! Please, I'll get your money later today! Just don't kill me, man!" The man continued begging for his life.

Roscoe kicked him in the stomach. Then he stood over his body as the man lay on the floor curled up in pain.

"Please don't hurt 'im!" his girlfriend tearfully shouted.

"Bitch, shut the fuck up!" Damon said, pointing his 9 mm at her head.

"Damon, go in there and kill that motherfucking baby! They think this is a joke?" Roscoe said.

"No! Please, not my baby!" the girl stood up and screamed.

"Please, Roscoe. What do you want? Just name it and you can have it. Just don't hurt my son, man!" the man desperately pleaded.

Damon stopped walking toward the bedroom and turned around. They had no intention on hurting the child. This was all a part of their devious plan.

"Anything?" Roscoe asked.

"Anything. Just don't hurt my son. Please!"

"Okay, then, Joe. Let me have *her* and we'll call it a deal. Afterward, I'll go my way, and you don't owe me shit. We'll be even!" Roscoe said.

"Please, man! Not my girl. I'll pay you all your money with interest," Joe said in a scared voice.

"Joe, just let me do it and get it over with!" the girl cried out.

"Keisha, no!" Joe said.

"Damon, I'm tired of playing with these two; go kill the kid!" Roscoe said in a serious tone.

"No! I'll do it! I'll do it! Just don't touch my baby!" Keisha begged.

"Joe, it's up to you. What's it gonna be?" Roscoe asked.

Joe lay on the floor crying and shaking his head. He was between a rock and a hard place.

"Just you, right?" he muttered.

"No, nigga! First me, then Damon. Then we'll leave, and you won't ever see us again," Roscoe said.

"Please, man. I'll get you your money, Roscoe!" Joe said.

"Joe, this is my last fucking time asking you. Your bitch's pussy or your baby's life!" Roscoe said angrily.

"Okay, go ahead," he muttered through falling tears.

"What did you say?" Roscoe asked with a sly grin on his face.

"Go ahead. Just go and get it over with!" Joe said softly, defeated.

Roscoe looked over at Keisha and smiled. Keisha was a dark-skinned female with average looks, but she had a body out of this world. From the first moment Roscoe and Damon saw her body, they wanted to fuck her. That's why they kept loan-sharking Joe's money, knowing that he wouldn't be able to pay it all back. Then they would have an excuse to go after his girl, Keisha.

"Watch this bitch-ass nigga, Damon. If he moves, put a hole in his head," Roscoe ordered, grabbing Keisha by her arm and walking her to the bedroom. When they entered the bedroom, the baby was still asleep inside the crib. Keisha went to shut the door, but Roscoe stopped her.

"Leave it open."

Keisha shook her head and started undressing. Roscoe went into his jeans pocket and took out a condom. A confused look came to Keisha's face. Right then, she realized that it was all a setup. She just wanted it all over with so she kept on undressing. When she had taken all of her clothes off, Roscoe just stared at her gorgeous black body. Keisha's measurements were 40DD-26-38. He walked over to her, then slid down his jeans. His dick was rock hard. He slid the condom on and then pushed Keisha back onto the bed.

"Please, let me just take my baby in the other room," she pleaded.

"The baby is fine!" Roscoe said climbing on top of her body and forcing his dick into her pussy.

"Ahhh! Ohhh!" she grunted. Keisha tried to hold back her loud groans, but she couldn't. Roscoe had her legs up high in the air, stroking in and out of her pussy with all his force.

"Ahhh! Yhhh! Ummm!" she moaned, cried out, and grunted all at once. Roscoe turned her around and started fucking her from behind.

"Ohhh! Ummm!" Tears fell down her scared face. In the other room, Joe lay on the floor in tears. He could hear everything going on. The sexual sounds of his woman being fucked in the nest room had him losing his mind. Damon stood over him, smiling and pointing the loaded gun at his head.

"Ahhh! God!" Keisha continued to cry out.

Roscoe was so turned on that his dick didn't go down after he had come in the condom. As he kept going, sweat dripped down his dark face. After he had finally finished, he threw the condom on the floor, then pulled up his jeans. Keisha was lying on the bed in tears, her pussy totally violated. When Roscoe left the room, Damon quickly walked in behind him. He was already turned on from hearing all of her moans and cries. Damon took a condom from out of his jeans and slid it on his already rock-hard dick.

"Can you just wait one minute?" Keisha asked, holding her stomach.

"Bitch, shut up!" Damon yelled, climbing on her body and ramming his dick inside of her. For the next thirty minutes, he fucked Keisha even more aggressively than Roscoe had.

"Ohh! Ahhh!" Keisha yelled out in pain.

When Roscoe and Damon finally left the apartment, Keisha had been brutally raped twice. Joe felt total humiliation. Their one-year-old child somehow was still sleeping peacefully.

While India was typing on her computer, she reached for her ringing cell phone. "Hello," she said.

"What's up, pretty?" Ricky asked.

"Hey, Ricky, did you get my message I left on your voice mail earlier?" India asked.

"Yeah, I heard it, and I'll be ready for my blind date with the lucky contest winner next Friday," he said, walking out of the gym and getting in his car.

"So what's up, Ricky?"

"Pretty, I need a big favor from you," he said, pulling off down the street.

"Anything," India said quickly.

"Girl, you better stop telling me 'anything,'" Ricky said laughing.

"Why? I mean it," India said seriously.

Ricky just laughed it off and said, "India, I wanted to ask you if you would mind taking Asia out this Saturday. She likes you a lot and—"

"Yeah, I'll go by your parents' house and pick her up Saturday around ten," India said, cutting him off in midspeech. "I love your beautiful little daughter. So, sure, she can hang out with me," India said excited and with a big smile.

"Thanks, India. How much do you want? I'll pay you," Ricky said driving his car down Belmont Avenue.

"Ricky, you know you don't have to pay me for taking your daughter out. Just don't let my mother find out, that's all. I don't want to hear her mouth," India said.

"You got it. Just like the last time, it will only be between me and you."

"And Asia," India added.

"Yeah, and Asia too," Ricky laughed. "Where's Nancy?"

"She's upstairs knocked out."

"This time of the day?" Ricky asked shocked.

"Yeah, she was out all night. She came in the house early this morning and went straight up into her bedroom and shut herself inside."

"The world is coming to an end. Nancy Robinson is not counting or collecting money. This can't be real," Ricky joked as they both starting laughing.

"So you told Asia that you didn't have a boyfriend, huh?" Ricky asked, quickly changing the subject.

"She told you that?" India said, feeling a little embarrassed.

"My baby tells me everything," he said joking.

"Well, it's the truth."

"What happened to your little boyfriend you had from college?" Ricky asked, turning his BMW down City Line Avenue.

"Too many headaches, too much stress, too much boy, not enough man!"

"Sorry to hear that."

"Don't be, 'cause I'm not!"

"Don't worry, a girl as pretty as you are won't have a problem finding a boyfriend," Ricky said teasing.

"I'm not looking for any boyfriend, Ricky; I'm looking for a man! A husband! A soul mate," India said seriously.

"You're too young to be thinking about all of that."

"Ricky, I told you before, I'm a full-grown woman. Ain't nothing about me young."

"Is that right?"

"That's right!"

"I hear you, pretty," Ricky said with a smile.

"And I hope I'm loud and clear," India said into the phone.

Chapter Eighteen

A True Friend

After Ricky finished talking to India, he checked all the other messages on his voice mail. He had over ten messages, all from different women. When he had heard the urgent message from his friend Carmen, he quickly called her and told her to meet him inside her building's parking garage. When Ricky pulled into the garage, he saw Carmen standing next to her Mercedes. He pulled his car beside her, and she quickly got inside and shut the door.

"What's wrong with you?" he asked, looking into her face.

"Ricky, this guy has been stalking me!" Carmen said, terrified.

"What guy?" he asked, concerned.

"Some guy I met one night down at Tower Records on South Street," Carmen said. "At first, the guy seemed cool. That's why I gave him my cell phone number. We went out once; he took me to dinner at Red Lobster. After dinner, we went back to his apartment to just chill. No sex. I just really wanted to chill; you know, watch a movie and just talk to each other. Anyway, while we were watching the movie, this guy falls asleep on the couch. I needed to use the bathroom, so I got up and walked down the hallway toward the bathroom."

"Then what happened?" Ricky asked, seeing the tears falling down Carmen's face.

"When I walked past his bedroom, I just happened to take a peek inside." Carmen wiped her tears and shook her head.

"Carmen, will you tell me what happened?" Ricky asked impatiently and frustrated.

"Ricky, this sick motherfucker had pictures all over his bedroom of me *naked*. He had cut my head from out of magazines I had posed for and placed my head on naked women's bodies. There were pictures of me all over the bedroom. Big ones, little ones, and they were all *naked* photos. I didn't even get to use the bathroom. I just tiptoed my ass right past the guy while he was still sleeping. I went out the door, got in my car, and drove off."

"What's this guy's name?"

"His name is Calvin, and he works down at the Tower Records."

"How long has this guy been stalking you?"

"Just a few days. He called my cell phone over a hundred times yesterday and twenty-five times already this morning.

"The nigga said he loves me. He said when I was a video model, that he was my number one fan."

"Does he know where you live?"

"No. You're the only person who knows where me and Hardrock live, but early this morning, I believe I saw Calvin inside his blue Maxima following me from the supermarket. I made sure I lost him before I came back home."

"Carmen, how do you keep getting yourself into situations like this? What if this crazy-ass nigga would've kidnapped you and held you hostage, or killed you in that house? So you haven't contacted the police or anything, right?" Ricky asked concerned.

"Ricky, I get tired of being stuck up in an apartment all day long, or hanging out with the same females all the time! I'm from New Jersey, and my man stays either on tour or is in some studio. I get lonely sometimes, and the only real friend I have is you. I haven't called the police. It's my fault that I'm in this mess, Ricky. I don't want Hardrock to find out about this," she cried.

Ricky reached over and wiped Carmen's tears from her face. "Carmen, you need to just slow down, shorty. You're engaged to one of the most successful rap artists in the country. But you can't keep meeting people and giving your number out to dudes because you 'get lonely' once in a while. Even if it is just to pass time. Do you even love Hardrock?"

"I don't know! I'm just so confused with everything right now," she said softly.

"Well, I'm telling you this, Carmen, if you don't love the man, then don't even play yourself or Hardrock and go through with the marriage. Many people make that mistake and end up regretting it in the long run. Look at all the signs first. Then, weigh all of your options before you say 'I do.' Carmen, if you think you're hurting now, marriage to the wrong man will only destroy you," he said seriously.

"What if I told you that I love you?" Carmen said, staring into Ricky's eyes.

"I'm positive that you have some love for me, Carmen, but it's not the love that you think it is. Our entire relationship has been based on sex. We don't know each other on no other level but sexual. We don't love each other, we *lust* each other. Most people who lust will lie to the people they really love just to keep on lusting."

Carmen sat there shaking her head. She knew everything that Ricky said was true. Ricky grabbed her hands. She looked deep into his serious eyes and started crying again.

"Carmen, don't worry about this guy Calvin. I'm gonna take care of everything. But from now on, shorty, I want you to start evaluating your life. You're a very beautiful woman. Don't let them niggas dog you or break you down, Carmen. And please don't be the cause of your own downfall, because believe it or not, so many good women are."

Carmen leaned over and gave Ricky a long, warm hug. A part of her wanted to hold on forever and never let him go. Ricky was like no other man she had ever met, and one of the few men that truly cared about her well-being. Ricky took out his cell phone and dialed a number. A male answered on the second ring.

"Hello."

"Thunder, it's me, Ricky. I need you to meet me down at the Tower Records on South Street in about half an hour," Ricky said.

"Drama?" Thunder asked, excited.

"Yeah, but it ain't nothing real major. Some punk who works there has been stalking a friend of mine."

"A pervert, pussy chaser. No more needs to be said. I'm on my way there," Thunder said hanging up the phone.

"Stop crying, shorty. Everything is going to be okay. You owe me for this," Ricky said with a smile, driving out of the parking garage.

"Don't worry. I'm looking forward to paying my debts," Carmen teased back.

While Ricky navigated his BMW through the congested City Line Avenue traffic, Carmen turned on the CD player and let the melodic, soulful voices of Jagged Edge take her far away.

On the corner of Sixteenth & Ellsworth, South Philly

Flex saw Roscoe's Escalade pull up and park. He quickly got out of his car and ran over to the truck and got inside.

"What's up, Roscoe? What took you so long?" Flex asked.

"We was down at the Tasker Home Projects taking care of some very important business," Roscoe laughed.

"Yeah and somebody had to get fucked, literally, for not paying their debt," Damon added, laughing.

Flex went into his jacket pocket and took out a thick roll of money.

"Damn, you ain't playing up in that club!" Roscoe said.

"Man, them kids is eating up those X-pills," Flex said with a smile.

"Just make sure you watch yourself. If you ever get caught with them pills, you'll be looking at a lot of time," Roscoe warned, passing Flex a small brown paper bag.

"Don't worry about me, Roscoe. I got this," Flex said while rushing out of the truck. Roscoe and Damon watched him get into his car and speed away.

"So what's up now? What we gonna do next?" Damon asked.

"We going to North Philly to go see Ronny. It's time for him to pay his overdue tab. Let's hope he ain't got it, because his girlfriend has a phat ass better than Keisha's," Roscoe said, as they both started laughing. Roscoe turned down Broad Street and headed toward North Philadelphia with money, lust, and sex on his evil mind.

When Carmen walked into the crowded Tower Records music store on South Street, she was nervous as hell. Before she had gone into the music store, Ricky and

Thunder had told her what to do. And once Carmen did her job, they would take care of the rest. Calvin spotted Carmen as soon as she walked through the door. He laid down a box of new CDs and quickly approached her. Carmen stood there with a big fake smile on her face.

"So you finally got tired of me chasing you, huh?" Calvin asked with a smile.

"I just wanted to see just how persistent you really were. A girl can't be too easy," she smiled.

"Why didn't you wake me up the other night before you left my apartment?" he asked seriously.

"You were sleeping, and I didn't want to wake you up."

"I've been calling you for days," Calvin said, agitated.

"I'm sorry, but I've been real busy. When can you get a break? I really need to talk to you."

"I can take a break now. I'm the assistant manager," he said proudly.

"I have my new truck parked around the corner. Can we go talk for a few minutes?" she asked.

"Yeah, let's go," Calvin said, excited.

When they walked outside, Carmen noticed Calvin's blue Maxima parked right out front. She was sure that it was the same car that had followed her from the supermarket earlier.

The big blue Excursion they walked to had dark tint on all the windows.

"That's a big-ass truck!" Calvin exclaimed.

"Oh, I can handle it. The bigger the better," she smiled. She walked around and used the key to get inside.

When she popped the lock up, Calvin quickly climbed in. Before he could say a word, the doors locked and a large arm wrapped tightly around his skinny neck. Thunder had been lying down in the backseat hiding behind the front passenger seat. He had Calvin gripped inside his huge arms. Calvin was struggling just to breathe. Carmen quickly pulled off down the street. Ricky pulled off right behind them. Calvin's face was red as an apple. The more he struggled, the more he could feel all the air leaving his body. He finally just let his hands fall to his side and gave up.

Five minutes later, Carmen pulled up into a secluded area, behind an old warehouse on Third Street. The warehouse was run-down and empty. After she parked, Ricky parked beside her and quickly got out of his car. He ran over and opened the passenger door. He grabbed Calvin's legs and dragged him out of the truck. Then Thunder got out of the truck and started stomping Calvin with his boots. Ricky joined in. After stomping him into a bloody mess, Thunder picked up his bruised body and held him while Ricky beat the hell out of him with his two fists. Calvin's face was bloody and swollen beyond recognition. Ricky had broken his jaw, some teeth, and one of his ribs.

"Carmen, come here!" Ricky yelled.

Carmen got out of the truck and walked up to him. Ricky grabbed Calvin's hair and lifted his beaten face.

"Do you see this woman, motherfucker?" Ricky asked angrily.

"Yelth. Yelth, mhan," Calvin muttered with his broken jaw.

"If you *ever* call her again, or if you *ever* follow her again, the next time, we won't be so nice," Ricky warned. "You hear me, motherfucker?"

"Yelth, I hwear ywou!" Calvin muttered in pain.

Thunder released Calvin's beaten body, then kicked him hard in his ass. Calvin's broken, bloody body slumped on the ground. Blood was flowing from his nose, eyes, and mouth. When he heard the two vehicles pull off, he was too beat up to get off the ground. As he lay there on the cold ground, Calvin knew that he would never bother Carmen again. She was the last person he ever wanted to see.

***

"Thanks, big guy. I'll talk to you later," Ricky said closing his cell phone. Ricky watched as Thunder made a right turn at the corner and drove in the opposite direction. He looked over at Carmen's smiling face.

"Thanks, Ricky," she said.

"Don't worry about it, pretty. You just remember what I said and stay focused out on these crazy streets," he warned.

"Since it's only 2:05, and you don't have to pick up your daughter until 3:15, let's swing by your spot. I can clean that blood off your hands," she said.

"And that's it?" he asked.

"No, but since we won't have enough time to get all freaky like we usually do, I'm gonna do that trick you like with my tongue," she teased.

"Which one?"

"The one that makes all your toes curl," Carmen said with a smile.

Chapter Nineteen

When Trouble Comes

Friday afternoon, inside a small house in North Philly

"Shut up, you stupid bitch!" Roscoe said, smacking the scared female to the floor.

"Please, Roscoe, I'ma get you all your money! I get my welfare check next week!" she cried.

"Bitch, you told me that same fucking story last week," Roscoe said, reaching down and squeezing his hand around her skinny throat. With an evil look on his face, he tightened his grip as hard as he could. The woman grabbed on his arm trying to loosen his grip, but he was too strong. When Roscoe finally let go of her throat, the woman started gasping for air. Her eyes were watery and red. Damon was standing there laughing. Both men had a thing for seeing women tortured and in pain. Roscoe punched the woman in her already swollen left eye. Once again she fell hard to the floor.

"Why do I have to pay my husband's debt?" she cried.

"'Cause that punk-ass nigga got locked up, still owing me my money!" Roscoe yelled angrily.

"Well, how much more do I have to pay? I fucked you. I sucked both of your dicks, and I gave you money!" she cried out.

"Bitch, your man owes me $3,500. You gave me $200, some worn-out pussy, and me and my friend a sorry-ass blowjob! I told that nigga right in front of you, if he fucks up my money, *you* would be the one who paid the cost."

"But he got locked up!" she protested.

"Tough motherfucking cookie! I want my money, bitch. I don't care if you have to get out and sell pussy on Broad Street!

"Get my fucking money, and if you try to run and hide again, the next time I track you down will be the last time. I'll be back in a few days, and you better have me some money," Roscoe threatened as he and Damon walked out the front door.

The scared woman sat there on the floor crying. She knew that Roscoe would be back when he said. And if she didn't have some money for him, things would be a lot worse.

Roscoe pulled off down the street in his truck.

"Man, you just dogged that bitch!" Damon said laughing.

"Fuck them bitches, man! I don't have no soft spots for those hoes! The only bitch I care about is my own, and I got her in total check," he bragged. "The rest of those bitches ain't got nothing coming; I treat 'em just like I do niggas."

"So what's next? The first two stops turned out to be fun!" Damon expressed.

"We're going to Chester, PA. I gotta go meet Robin on Ninth Street. She left a message on my voice mail."

"What she say?"

"She said that she got all my money."

"Smart girl," Damon laughed.

West Philly, Forty-ninth Street and Fairmount

Twist was standing in the doorway of his house when Ricky pulled up in his BMW and parked. Twist walked over to the car with three CDs in his hand. He passed them to Ricky and said, "Ricky, I hooked those CDs up, man. I got everybody on that list you gave me. You got over six hours of nonstop, baby-making music, man!"

"Did you get Earth, Wind and Fire?" Ricky asked.

"Man, I told you, I got everybody. With my computer, I can get anybody's songs. You got Donny Hathaway, Luther, Gerald Levert, Al B. Sure!, Rose Royce, Keith Sweat, Boyz II Men, Stylistics, Dru Hill, New Edition, Blackstreet, Guy, Teddy Pendergrass, O'Jays, R. Kelly, Chico DeBarge, Maxwell, Musiq, Jill Scott—"

"All right, Twist, I got it," Ricky said, cutting him off.

"So who's the lucky girl?" Twist asked.

"Guess," Ricky smiled.

"Come on, man. I'll be standing here guessing all night."

"Roscoe's fiancée," Ricky said seriously.

"What? No way!" Twist laughed. "The pretty little redbone who be coming to all of your shows?"

"Yeah, she's meeting me at my loft right after I go pick my daughter, yo, and drop her off at home."

"Man, Roscoe loves that girl. He waits outside the club for her every Monday and Wednesday. And I saw that big-ass rock on her finger! Oh shit," Twist said, jumping up and down like a little kid. "Why you seeing her so early?"

"Because she took off of work today without Roscoe knowing about it. He picks her up at her job every night at 10:00. I told her that I needed a good amount of time with her before she meets Roscoe back at the hospital where she works."

"Man, this is crazy. No wonder you wanted those CDs bad," Twist said seriously.

Ricky stuck his fist out the window and gave Twist a pound. After rolling his window up, he beeped his horn and slowly pulled off down the street. Twist stood there in total disbelief. Ricky didn't feed into Roscoe's game of violence. What Ricky did was a far more skillful tactic. He went after his enemy's only weakness: his beautiful, young fiancée, Tori, the true love of Roscoe's life. So while Roscoe was stuck on doing battle with Ricky, Ricky had strategically put a plan together to win the whole war. His lifelong enemy would never see it coming, because there are no rules in love and war.

A few hours later

After leaving Chester, PA, where Roscoe picked up some money that was owed, he and Damon drove across the Benjamin Franklin Bridge to Camden, New Jersey. After shaking down a few people in Jersey, they crossed over the bridge to Philly and drove to Germantown.

Roscoe and Damon were inside a house on Chew Avenue talking to a guy. The guy's name was Troy. He was known as the person who could get any kind of handgun on the black market. Down in the basement of the house, Troy, Roscoe, and Damon sat around a large, brown box of new guns. Inside the box was a 9 mm with attached silencer, .380s, .40, .45, .357s, .38s, and boxes of ammo. While Troy was negotiating a price for the large shipment of guns, Roscoe gave Damon a sneaky wink.

"So what do you want for the whole box?" Roscoe asked.

"That's seventy-five handguns and boxes of bullets," Troy said.

"How much, man?" Roscoe asked again.

"Give me $200 for each gun. Now, that's a deal. That's only $15,000. You'll double that on the streets."

"What's up with those silencers? Do they work?" Damon asked, picking up two 9 mm silencers. He tossed one over to Roscoe. Troy walked over by the wall and picked up a shot-up mannequin. He used it for all the gun customers who bought silencers from him.

Roscoe and Damon loaded their clips and walked over to Troy and the mannequin.

"Go ahead and shoot. You'll see those silencers are the top of the line." Troy stood the mannequin up and stepped away. Damon aimed the gun at the mannequin and squeezed twice.

Shh! Shh! The bullets were quiet, but the powerful force knocked the mannequin to the floor.

"I told you, man, y'all ain't heard nothing!" Troy bragged.

"Your turn, Roscoe," he said, walking over and standing the mannequin back up. Roscoe pointed the gun at the mannequin and laughed.

"What's wrong?" Troy asked.

Turning, Roscoe pointed the gun at Troy's head and said, "Nothing, you stupid motherfucker!" Then he squeezed the trigger.

Shh! Shh!

Damon shot Troy three more times in the head. Troy's body stopped moving. Roscoe and Damon quickly grabbed the entire box of guns and carried them upstairs. After putting the box of guns in the back of Roscoe's Escalade, they sped off. For them, today had been a perfect day. Three women had been beaten, three others had paid their debts, one man beat down severely, and now another one dead. On top of all that, they came away with seventy-five brand-new guns and ammo. On their way back to West Philly, they smoked on a fat blunt and laughed.

Chapter Twenty

"Mr. Orgasm"

Pure bliss

When Ricky had pulled up in front of his loft, Tori was already standing outside waiting. She was looking even prettier than the last time he had seen her. When Ricky got out of his car, nervousness swept through Tori's entire body. She was nervous more than she had ever been in all her life—and just as scared. Even with all the nervousness, her body was still burning with desire. Tori was dressed in a pair of tight-fitting jeans that made her nice round ass stick out even more. Her hair was done up in a long braided ponytail that hung down her back. She was wearing a tan-colored Versace jacket and a pair of matching Versace sandals.

When they walked into the loft, she was in total amazement. It was laid out like one of those expensive condos she had seen in magazines. Without any words being spoken, Ricky grabbed her hand and walked her back into his bedroom. When she saw the mirrors all over the walls, she just smiled and shook her head.

"Take off your clothes and get relaxed. I'll be right back," he said, walking out of the bedroom.

Tori sat on the edge of the bed and took off her jacket. The nervousness was slowly subsiding. As she began taking off the rest of her clothes and shoes, music started flowing out of the speakers. When Ricky walked back into the room, he held two glasses of white Zinfandel in his hands. Tori just sat there smiling. Her blouse and jeans were still on.

"I want you to stand up and take everything off."

"Everything?" she said softly.

"Everything!" Ricky said in a serious voice.

Tori stood up from the bed and started to slowly undress. Ricky watched as she unbuttoned her blouse and laid it on the carpeted floor. Then she slid off her jeans, bra, and thong. He stood there staring at her beautiful, petite body. From head to toe, she was a work of fine art. He walked up to her and passed her the glass of wine.

"Now, go lie back on my bed and relax," he instructed.

Tori climbed on the large king-size bed and got comfortable. She sat there sipping on the wine, watching Ricky's every move. Her nervousness was now a forgotten memory. Wetness was building up inside of her love tunnel. She sipped and watched Ricky slowly undress in front of her. When he was totally naked, she just sat there in amazement. He had the perfect body, she thought. He was chiseled to perfection with muscles in all the right places. And the man was hung like a horse.

"Oh my God!" Tori softly muttered to herself. She quickly sipped down the rest of her wine and just shook her head.

"The reason why I told you to get undressed was because when you're around me, I want you to be totally free with your body. In order for us to reach that ultimate level, we must first be on the same page," he said.

After Ricky finished his wine, he placed both of the empty wineglasses on the floor. Then he told Tori to lie on her stomach across the bed. She did as he told her without protest. Ricky reached under a pillow and took out a small bottle of peach body lotion. After rubbing it on his hands, he sank his warm fingers into Tori's back.

"Now, just relax and let me take your mind, body, and soul far away," he said while massaging his strong hands into her soft, delicate skin.

As Ricky explored her body with his hands, Tori was lost in a world of passion and desire. From forehead to her pedicured toes, Ricky let his hands travel nonstop. He massaged her neck, upper and lower back, ass, thighs, shoulders, arms, and feet. Then he turned her over on her back and did the same to her breasts, erected nipples, face, all over her stomach, and the gold belly ring she had inside her navel. When Ricky had finally finished, he started kissing the nape of her neck and around her earlobes.

"Ohh!" she moaned.

Ricky moved his hand down to her wetness. With his fingers, he started light and high, slightly above Tori's sensitive clit, and started working his way down.

"Ohh! Yes! Ahhh!" she moaned.

When Tori leaned her body into him, that was the signal to let him know that he was stimulating the right spot. The feeling was so good that Tori had already come twice. Ricky found his way to the hidden G-spot. Tori had never known it existed. He rubbed his two fingers on her G-spot, watching as her body started trembling uncontrollably.

"Ahhh! I'm having an orgasm!" she yelled out in pleasure. Tori had just experienced her first G-spot orgasm. The feeling was so intense and powerful that she ejaculated from her pussy.

"Ohh! God!" she screamed.

The feeling inside her trembling body had her both excited and frightened at the same time. After that, Ricky grabbed a condom from under his pillow. He put it on his long, hard dick and turned Tori around on her stomach.

He pulled her body down to the edge of the king-size bed. Then he spread her legs wide apart. As her trembling body was still recovering from the amazing G-spot orgasm, Ricky eased his long, hard dick into the deepness of her throbbing wet walls. While he stroked long and hard, Tori moaned with joy and pain. Ricky grabbed her long braided ponytail and wrapped it around his hand.

"Ohh! I'm com . . . coming again!" she moaned. "Oh my God! I'm having another orgasm! God!" she cried out in pleasure. While Ricky kept stroking, tears of pure bliss fell from her eyes.

"Ahhh! Ohhh!" she grunted.

"Now, what's my name?" Ricky asked stroking harder.

"'Mr. Orgasm! Mr. Orgasm!' I'm . . . I'm . . . having another orgasm!" Tori screamed out. "Ahhhh!"

While the music on the CD played, Ricky never stopped stroking deep inside her wet pussy. Tori had already come more in less than one hour than she did the entire month with her fiancé. Ricky slid out his dick and spread out Tori's ass cheeks. He stuck his middle finger inside her pussy, and then slid it inside her asshole.

"Uhh!" she gasped. Her asshole was tight, but Ricky played inside of it with his finger until it loosened up.

"Please go slow. I never did it before," Tori moaned softly.

Ricky leaned down to her ear and whispered, "Don't worry, beautiful. 'Mr. Orgasm' is gonna take *good* care of you." Ricky slid out his finger, and then slowly eased his long, hard dick inside Tori's asshole as far as he could go.

"Ohhh! Ahhh! Mmmm!"

Ricky gripped her hips and started slowly stroking inside her.

"Oh God! Oh God! Oh God!" Tori grunted out every time he pushed and pulled.

"Now, what's my name?"

"'Mr. Orgasm!' Your name is 'Mr. Orgasm! Mr. Orgasm!'" Tori cried out as another orgasm swept throughout her body. She could only lie there in tears as her body had just experienced her first ever anal orgasm. Tori couldn't believe the feelings that had taken total control over her body. She had come so many times that a large stain covered the silk sheets. Ricky slid his dick out of her ass and turned her around on her back.

"Now, I want you to watch me fuck your brains out," he said, putting her legs over his broad shoulders. Then Ricky placed a pillow underneath her hips so it could increase the pressure on her clit and allow deeper penetration. He slid his stiff shaft in as far as he could go. Now he started fucking Tori aggressively. She moaned, grunted, and cried, all at the same time.

"What's my name?"

"'Mr. Orgasm! Mr. Orgasm! Mr. Orgasm!'" Tori screamed out. Before they had finished, Ricky had fucked Tori in every position known to man. He fucked her all over his loft. The living room, dining room, shower, floor, couch, and on all the tables. Tori had come so much that she started begging Ricky to stop. She had gotten the sex lesson 101 of her life. Ricky stood there watching as Tori lay on the living-room floor, crying in the fetal position.

"What's wrong?" he asked.

Tori looked into his caring eyes and tearfully said, "I can't believe you just fucked me like that!"

Ricky leaned over and kissed her forehead. "Believe it. Because it only gets better," he said, lying down beside her. While Tori lay there trembling, Ricky rubbed her back and wiped away her tears.

Chapter Twenty-One

Everybody Has a Weakness

Later that night

DJ Twist had the club jumping. His mixing and scratching skills were one of a kind. A group of female fans stood around the booth. He enjoyed showing off his skills when people were watching. The club was packed with young men and women who had come out to have a good time. Big Nook had already thrown out three people for fighting. Some people just couldn't come out to the club without getting into a fight. But Big Nook and his security crew weren't having it! He and India were standing on the balcony talking.

"I talked to Asia earlier today on the phone. She's excited about me coming to get her in the morning," India said with a big grin.

"You seem more excited than probably she is," Big Nook said.

"I am. Asia is a beautiful little girl, and I really feel a strange connection with her." India looked up at Big Nook and saw his eyes focused on the crowd. When she followed his stare, she saw that he was watching Flex.

"Big Nook, what do you think is up with Flex?"

"Huh?" he said, snapping out of his stare.

"I said what's up with Flex? He's got so many older women chasing after him on male stripper night, but he's here at the club faithfully on all of our hip-hop nights."

"Maybe Flex like 'em young."

"I just don't understand why a grown-ass man wanna be around eighteen- and nineteen-year-old kids all night. There's something about him I just don't like," India said seriously.

"Me too," Big Nook said with a disgusted look on his face.

"Flex, do you got a minute?" the skinny white kid said tapping on his shoulder. When Flex turned around and saw who it was, he smiled.

"Ladies, I'll be right back," Flex said before walking through the crowd with the skinny white guy. He found a secluded spot in the back of the club.

"Bobby, what's up, man? How many do you need?" Flex asked.

"I need twenty more. You got it?"

"Do I got it? Man, I keep it," Flex said going into his jacket pocket and taking out a clear Ziploc bag. The bag was filled with Ecstasy pills. After Flex had counted out twenty pills, he passed them to Bobby. Bobby paid Flex with the marked money that Hightower had given him.

"Man, what do you be doing with all those pills? You're my number one customer," Flex said.

"The ones that I don't use, I sell to my friends," Bobby replied, showing his mouth full of braces.

"Well, maybe we can hook up, and you start working for me," Flex offered. "I could us somebody like you."

"Hey, I'll think about it, Flex. Maybe we can hook up one day soon."

"All right, Bobby. Just think about it. I'll see you later. I have to get back over to my two little cuties," Flex said giving him a pound and walking away. Bobby smiled as he watched Flex maneuver his way through the crowd. Once again, he had everything that Flex said recorded on tape.

When Tori walked into the apartment, Roscoe was sitting on the sofa waiting for her. It was 1:27 a.m.

"Where the fuck you been all day long?" he asked angrily. "Why wasn't you at work when I went by there to pick you up? And why didn't you let me know you took off today? What the fuck is going on, Tori?" Roscoe stood up and shouted.

"Roscoe, sit down. We need to talk," Tori said softly. She walked over and sat down on the sofa, but she didn't take off her coat.

"Tori, what the fuck is going on?"

"Will you please sit down? I told you that we need to talk," she said in a serious voice.

Roscoe looked into Tori's eyes and sat back down beside her. She saw confusion on his face.

"Why didn't you call me or answer your cell phone? I left two messages on your voice mail. I was worried about you. When I talked to Malinda, she told me that she didn't see you all day. What's going on?" he asked in a concerned voice.

Tori sat there shaking her head. Tears were falling from her eyes. She reached into her pocket and took out the 3-carat diamond engagement ring.

"Here, Roscoe. I don't think I'm gonna be needing this anymore," she said, passing Roscoe the ring.

"What? What the fuck is you talking about?" he yelled.

"Roscoe, I think we need a break. I don't think I'm ready for marriage or a commitment like that right now. That's why I decided to move out of the apartment until I get my mind right. I'm sorry, but that's how I truly feel."

"Are you fucking kidding me? We've been together for three-and-a-half years! I took you outta those run-down Forty-sixth Street Projects and moved you into this expensive-ass apartment! I buy and give you everything you want! I sent you to nursing school! Paid your whole tuition! And you got the nerve to come in here at 1:30 in the fucking morning telling me you need a fucking break? Bitch, is you crazy?" he screamed out angrily.

Tori looked up at him with a disgusted expression on her face. It was the first time that Roscoe ever saw that expression. It was also the first time that Roscoe had ever called her a bitch. The two things that he had never done to Tori was to call her out of her name or put his hands on her. Tori had a hold on Roscoe's heart that couldn't be broken loose. She was the true love of his life, and now her painful words had him feeling like his heart was breaking into a thousand little pieces.

"Roscoe, I will always have love for you, but right now, I just gotta follow my heart! And until I can get my mind right, I think it's best that we stay away from each other," she said seriously.

"Is it another guy?" Roscoe muttered as the tears welled up in his eyes.

"No. I've thought about this for a while now," she lied.

"Come on, baby, can't we just talk about this?" he pleaded, trying his best to control his tears.

"I'm sorry, Roscoe, but it's just not working anymore," Tori stood up and sadly said.

"You fucked somebody else, didn't you?" Roscoe asked. "That's it, ain't it?"

Tori looked deep into his crying eyes and saw pain all over his face. She had never seen Roscoe cry before. Never seen him so weak. So broken.

"No, Roscoe I didn't fuck nobody," she lied with a straight face. "I'm going to get my suitcase and pack me up a few things. I'll get the rest of my belongings in a few days. I'm . . . I'm sorry, Roscoe," Tori said walking away.

Roscoe stood there watching her walk into the bedroom. He was confused beyond all words. He was trying to figure how they'd gotten to this point. He wasn't ready to lose her, but he wasn't about to beg someone to stay that didn't want to. In his heart, he didn't feel like he'd done anything that was this detrimental. He hadn't felt this way about anyone in a very long time. His heart was breaking. As he sat there shattered inside, Tori walked out of the bedroom carrying her suitcase full of clothes. Roscoe was sitting on the sofa crying with his head down.

After a long sigh, Tori wiped away her tears and said, "I'll be back in a few days to come get the rest of my stuff. Don't call me on my cell phone 'cause I'm changing the number tomorrow. I'll call you. Bye, Roscoe." She turned around and walked out the front door.

Roscoe didn't say a word when she left the apartment. His mind was too lost to comment. The woman whom he had loved more than anything in the world had looked into his eyes and told him that it was over. That she needed a "break." The pain filled his entire body. As the tears continued to fall, he looked over at the 3-carat diamond engagement ring that was lying all alone on the coffee table. He realized at this moment that all of his dreams had just walked right out the door.

A half hour later, a yellow cab pulled up in front of Ricky's loft. Ricky was standing in the doorway with only his silk Gucci robe on and matching slippers. He walked over to the cabbie and gave him a twenty-dollar bill.

"Keep the change," he said. Ricky opened the door and grabbed the suitcase. Tori looked into his handsome face and smiled.

She got out of the cab and walked over to him.

“Did you handle your business?” he asked, walking toward the front door.

“Yes. I took care of what I needed to,” she replied, following Ricky into the loft.

Ricky looked into her eyes and said, “You been crying, I see.”

“What I had to do was hard, but at the same time, I feel like it was needed,” she said softly.

Ricky set the suitcase down and walked up to her. “Just follow your heart, pretty.”

“I did,” she muttered softly. “So, you gonna drop me off at my mother’s house in the morning, right?”

“I told you that I would do it. I’ll drop you off on my way to go see my daughter,” Ricky said.

Sighing, Tori said, “So what now?”

Ricky grabbed her in his arms and started passionately tonguing her down. He could feel her melting in his arms. He kissed her all over her face and neck. Tori just stood there, hypnotized by his presence. Once again, her body was burning with desire and lust.

“Go in my bedroom and take off all your clothes,” he said.

“I’m gonna get us some wine.”

Without any hesitation, Tori turned around and walked toward the bedroom.

Chapter Twenty-Two

Pleasure and Pain

Early Saturday morning

In the tranquility of his bedroom, Ricky and Tori had copulated all night long. After an early-morning shower together and a delicious breakfast that Ricky had cooked, he dropped her off at her mother's house. Before driving off, he kissed her on the lips and told her that he would see her soon. Then he drove straight to his parents' house in Wynnefield. When he pulled up in his car, India's red Range Rover was parked out front. India, Nicole, and Asia were all standing around talking. Asia ran over to her father and gave him a big hug.

"Hey, sweetie. You look pretty today," Ricky said, lifting her up in the air and swinging her around. After he put Asia down, he looked over at India. Like always, she was looking as fine as ever. Ricky let his eyes explore her body as India did the same.

"Daddy, Ms. India is taking me to the circus, and she's taking me shopping," Asia said ecstatically.

Ricky kneeled down and said, "You be a good girl, you hear me?"

"Yes, Daddy, I will," Asia promised with a big smile.

India looked at Ricky and said, "You have my cell phone number, and I have yours. If you want to call me and check up on her, please do. The circus is in town for a few days. I just wanted to take her there to have some fun. Then afterward, we're going downtown to the Gallery Mall."

"Maybe the next time I can go with y'all," Ricky said seriously.

"That would be nice. Very nice," India said with a smile.

Asia walked over to India and grabbed her hand. Ricky looked at them both smiling and felt a strange feeling inside his body. Nicole saw the way Ricky looked at India and just shook her head. She knew Ricky better than anybody. That's why when she looked into her brother's eyes, she saw the same way Ricky used to look at Asia's mother, Cheryl.

"Daddy, can you go with us?" Asia asked.

"No, sweetie, not today. I have a busy day ahead of me."

Asia frowned up her pretty little face. After they all walked out the door, Ricky watched as India and Asia got into the Range Rover. India strapped Asia in her seat belt. Nicole was standing in the doorway smiling and waving good-bye.

Ricky walked up to the window and said, "India, thank you for doing this—"

"Ricky, I told you, I enjoy being with Asia. She's a wonderful little girl. Plus, being with her takes a lot of things off my mind. One day I'm going to be a mother and being with Asia is giving me a lot of practice. Maybe if I can just meet that soul mate you asked me about the other night, things will start happening a lot sooner than later."

"So, that's all you're waiting for, huh?" Ricky asked seriously.

India had remembered her conversation with Big Nook and decided to pour it on.

"Ricky, I don't smoke or drink. I'm twenty-two years old. Single. I have a college degree. No children, and I'm God-fearing. Yes, my soul mate is who I'm waiting for.

A man who will teach me and complete me. I'm gonna love my man like he ain't never seen love before, and I will be my man's rock for life. So until I find me a good man who's willing to give himself to me completely, I'll continue to be by myself."

"You have a perfect résumé," he said.

"Yup, and it's all for the man who's willing to love me," India replied, starting up her SUV. "I'll have Asia back before 8:00 o'clock. I'll call you if I need to, and feel free to call me as well."

Ricky stood back on the sidewalk and waved as India and Asia drove away. After they left, he walked back into the house. Nicole was sitting on the sofa waiting for him.

"Big brother, you need to stop playing yourself and get with that woman. I saw the way y'all looked at each other, and I'm telling you, I know love when I see it. What are you waiting for, Ricky? Why ain't India your girlfriend?" she asked seriously.

"Because she can't be, that's why," he replied.

Nicole stood up from the sofa and walked over to him. She looked deep into Ricky's eyes. "The last time I saw that look in your eyes, you were with Cheryl. You ain't never let none of your other female friends take Asia out. I don't know why you're running from that girl, but I truly hope, Ricky, that you fix the problem and snatch India up before someone else do it for you." Nicole turned and walked away. When she got to the stairs, she turned around and said, "Oh, thanks for taking me to school and meeting Mrs. Langston. She was smiling all day long."

"I'm supposed to see her tonight. She invited me over to her house," Ricky said grinning.

"Okay, lover boy, I'll talk to you later. Just remember what I told you about India." she reminded him, walking up the stairs. When Nicole went upstairs into her bedroom, Ricky sat down on the sofa.

***

"I think my daddy likes you, Ms. India," Asia said.

India stopped the Range Rover at the red light and asked, "Why do you think that?"

"Because my daddy looks at you funny," Asia said with a smile.

"He does?"

"Yup. I mean, yes. He looks at you the same way he looks at my mother's old pictures," Asia smiled.

"Well, I like your daddy too," India said, pulling off when the light turned.

"Are you gonna be my stepmother one day?"

The question caught India completely off guard. "Would you like that?"

"Yup. I mean, yes, and I think my daddy would like it too," Asia said.

A few hours later

"Damn, he did all of that?" Malinda said shocked.

"I'm telling you, Malinda, the man is gifted!" Tori smiled.

"Girl, I still don't believe you walked out on Roscoe! That nigga was calling me all last night looking for you. I know he knew I was lying, but I told him every time he called the same thing. 'I ain't see her all day,'" Malinda said laughing. "Do you think Roscoe is gonna just let you go like that?" she said in a serious tone.

"He don't have a choice. I love Roscoe, but I'm not in love with him the way I should be to commit my life to him forever."

"Tori, I just don't understand how after three and a half years of being with somebody you can just easily walk away from them. What did 'Mr. Orgasm' do to you?" Malinda asked.

"Malinda, it's hard to explain. He did everything to me that Roscoe never did. It was so much deeper than just sex. The man had me screaming, yelling, crying, moaning—just from his kisses! I honestly didn't have any control of my own mind, body, and soul. And every time we finished making love, he would cuddle up with me and just talk to me," Tori said.

"Talk about what?" Malinda asked curiously.

"About life. About *my* life. The man is deep. He talked to me about learning to love myself first. And I could tell that he was sincere. I decided to leave Roscoe because being with Ricky showed me that I wasn't truly happy with the man I was engaged to. Not only sexually, but emotionally, mentally, and spiritually also. Roscoe only satisfies me financially. That's not enough anymore. I'm not no young, naïve little girl caught up in a materialistic lifestyle anymore. I'm a full-grown woman with needs. Why should I marry a man who doesn't even know the woman he has? My mistake was letting our relationship get this far without seeing the signs of misery sooner. Being with Ricky last night opened my confused eyes. Yes, I must admit that the sex was the best I ever had in my life, but his mind and presence played a major part too," Tori said seriously.

"So what's up with y'all now?" Malinda questioned.

"We are friends, and I think we will be friends for a very long time," Tori said.

"What about Roscoe?"

"I truly hope Roscoe finds what he's looking for, but that person will no longer be me. Like I said, I love Roscoe, and I always will for all the things he's done for me, but I am not in love with him like I thought I was, so I had to do what was good for me. I had to move on."

Malinda just shook her head in total disbelief. Then she looked at Tori and said, “Okay, enough of all that. Tell me more about the trick he did with his finger, his tongue, and the vibrator.” They both started laughing.

Chapter Twenty-Three

Love and Pain

India and Asia had enjoyed a wonderful time together at the circus. India let Asia ride on the pony, take pictures with the clowns, and even play with some of the other children that were there. They ate popcorn, cotton candy, corn dogs, and shared a large Pepsi and an order of fries. Most of the time they held hands and talked. Asia was having the time of her life. India was like her new best friend and role model. After they took some pictures together of their adventurous day at the circus, they got inside the Range Rover and India drove downtown to the Gallery Shopping Mall on Ninth and Market street. She took Asia to the GAP Kids outlet, KB toy store, and a few other stores. Carrying all the bags from their shopping spree, they rode the escalator up to the third-floor parking lot and put all of the shopping bags into the truck. Five minutes later, they were driving out of the Gallery Mall with a trunk full of new toys and clothes and big happy smiles on both their beautiful faces.

Damon looked at his friend Roscoe and didn't know what to say. He had never seen Roscoe so mad. So confused. They had been driving around the city all day long picking up money and beating people down. Roscoe was so upset about his breakup with Tori that he stomped a female worker's head into the ground until she fell unconscious. Throughout their violent journey, he had beaten down four different women and two men. When he decided to call Tori, she had already changed the number on her cell phone.

Roscoe looked over at Damon and said, "Tell me what you think, man."

After a long sigh, Damon said, "I honestly can't believe it! I can't understand why or what could make her just suddenly want to end y'all's relationship. You treat that girl like a queen. She don't need for nothing."

"Do you think she's been fucking around on me?" Roscoe muttered desperately.

"Naw, man! With who? Who is crazy enough to sleep around with Roscoe's fiancée? Plus, can't nobody give her nothing that you ain't already given her," Damon said, trying his best to cheer Roscoe up.

"I'm telling you, Damon, there's something going on, and I'm gonna find out what it is. If it's another man she leaving me for, I'll kill'em both before I let that happen," Roscoe said, punching his fist into the steering wheel.

"Well, if anybody know the truth, it's got to be Malinda. Girls talk, and they are best friends, so I'm sure Tori always confides in her. Plus, they work together at the hospital. If Tori won't tell you what's really going on, then maybe we might need to put the press down on Malinda," Damon said with a shady grin.

Roscoe just nodded his head. "I'ma wait awhile and see if Tori comes back. If not, we gonna pay Malinda a visit."

Chapter Twenty-Four

Desperate Housewives

Inside the Hyatt Regency Hotel, Flex and Nancy had just finished making love. Nancy had gotten the suite for the whole weekend. Throughout their stay, they would leave and go handle some business, then meet back later to make love. Nancy was lying across Flex's lap as he sat up on the bed watching the flat-screen TV.

"How long do we have to keep sneaking around?" he asked.

"Flex, I told you already, as long as it takes. My husband ain't even been dead a whole year yet. Do you know what that would look like? What will people think?" Nancy asked.

"Is that why you went and had the abortion? Because of what people think?" Flex asked angrily.

"Flex, I thought we moved past that. I'm almost fifty years old. What the hell would I look like having another baby? I was pregnant when my husband was still alive. How would that have looked? A baby would've messed up everything we put together. Who do you think the police would've been looking at first for my husband's murder? His adulterous wife and her handsome young lover!"

Nancy looked up at Flex's sad face and said, "Baby, just give it a little more time. At least six more months, then we'll come out in the open about our relationship.

And by then, I'll have a good excuse to get rid of Ricky so you can take his place as the club's new number one exotic dancer," she said, moving the sheet back and grabbing his hard dick.

"Now, why don't you just lie back and relax and let my warm mouth put you back to sleep," she said seductively.

Ricky pulled up in front of the beautiful row home and parked his BMW. The Art Museum section of the city was where the upper-middle-class citizens lived. The street was quiet, clean, and lined with tall trees. He got out of his car and walked up and knocked on the front door. Moments later, Victoria opened the door and let him inside. Ricky stood there with a shocked expression on his face. Victoria was wearing a short, pink, see-through nightie, with nothing on under it. Ricky could see her hairy pussy and her luscious breasts staring at him right in the face. Victoria had a gorgeous body that went perfect with her lovely face. The scent of her perfume and those ocean-green eyes had Ricky instantly turned on. He took off his quilted black leather jacket and passed it to her. Victoria took it and hung it up in a closet.

"Did you have a hard time finding the house?"

"No, your directions were perfect," he said, looking around the beautifully decorated home.

"Thirsty?"

"No, I'm fine," Ricky replied, looking into her eyes.

"What's wrong, handsome?" she asked.

"I'm trying to figure you out, that's all," he said seriously.

"What have you figured out so far?" she teased.

"I just don't understand why would a woman as beautiful and educated as yourself want to pay for sex. Is it that you want to sleep with a black man? Is it a fantasy of yours? What is it?" Ricky asked, confused.

Victoria looked at him and said, "Yes, it's both of the above, and a lot more also. I've always had fantasies about being with a black man. After I saw you dance in that club, I just couldn't get you outta my mind. I've left messages on your Web site's e-mail a few times. I even signed up for your 'Mr. Orgasm' Number One Fan Contest. When I found out that you were my student's older brother, I asked her to introduce me to you."

"Persistent, huh?" Ricky said, smiling.

"Very. When I see a good thing," Victoria flirted.

"So you've never been with a black man before?"

"Never," Victoria smiled.

"So you're just curious to see if the myth is true or not, huh?"

"No. I already know that the myth is true. All my girlfriends have black lovers or have slept with a black man before. I guess you can say that I'm just overdue," Victoria replied flirtatiously. She walked over to the glass coffee table and picked up five hundred-dollar bills.

"Here is the $500 you charged me."

Ricky folded the money and put it inside his pants pocket.

After Victoria walked around, dimming all the lights in the house, she grabbed Ricky's hand and said, "Come follow me. Up to my bedroom."

They walked up the stairs and entered a large, spacious bedroom. A canopy queen-size bed sat up against the wall. The bedroom was well decorated with a large walk-in closet. Victoria dimmed the bedroom light, then walked over to the stereo wall unit.

"Do you like Kenny G?" she asked softly.

"Yeah, Kenny G's fine," he replied, watching her from behind. After sliding the CD in, she pressed the *play* button, and Kenny G's magical soprano sax flowed from out of the speakers. She turned around and saw Ricky staring at her. She looked into his handsome dark face and bedroom eyes and smiled. Without saying another word, Victoria lifted her pink nightie over her head and tossed it on an empty chair.

"You like?" she asked, spinning around so Ricky could see her gorgeous hourglass figure. He just stood there in total amazement.

"Your turn," Victoria said invitingly. Ricky started slowly undressing. While he unbuttoned his shirt, Victoria stood there playing with her wet pussy. Ricky watched as she took her fingers out of her wetness and put them into her mouth. When he slid down his pants and boxers, Victoria looked at his mammoth dick and gasped. Ricky's eight-and-a-half-inch rock-hard dick was at full erection.

"Oh my God!" she muttered. Ricky had the biggest, baddest, blackest dick that she had ever seen. After a long sigh, Victoria walked over to the bed and lay her naked body across it. Ricky quickly joined her as he climbed on top of her excited body. He began kissing all over her neck and shoulders. While he kissed on her breasts, Victoria reached under the pillow and took out a condom.

"Here, big boy, it's a Magnum. Just like you asked for," she said. "Lie back and I'll put it on for you," Victoria said eagerly.

Ricky lay back and watched as Victoria ripped open the condom and slid it all the way down his dick. It was a perfect fit. He placed Victoria on her back and started kissing all over her body.

"Mmmm!" she moaned, as his lips maneuvered their way around her breasts. After kissing all over her body, Ricky grabbed a pillow and put it under her hips. He then spread open her legs and slid his hard dick into her wet pussy.

"Ahhhhhhhhhhh!" Victoria yelled out. He filled up her entire insides. "Ohh! Yesss! Yesss! Ohhh!" Victoria moaned out. Her body trembled under him. Her hands cupped his firm ass. Ricky stroked hard and long. For several minutes his superior sexual strength overpowered and overwhelmed her. Victoria screamed out as the powerful orgasm exploded all throughout her body. As Ricky continued on with his dominant sexual performance, the closet door slowly creeped open. Walking from the closet was an older, naked white man. Ricky saw the man standing there and quickly jumped up off of Victoria.

"What the fuck is going on?" Ricky asked in shock. "Who the fuck is you?" Ricky shouted.

"That's my husband!" Victoria said.

"I'm sorry if I scared you," the man said calmly.

"You been *watching* us?" Ricky asked, stunned.

"Yes. I saw everything," he said.

"Victoria, what the fuck is going on?" Ricky asked, walking over and picking up his pants.

"No, please, don't go, Ricky! This is my husband, Tom, and this was his fantasy too!" she revealed.

"What?"

"Today is Tom's birthday. He wanted to do something special. Something totally different," she said.

"You want to see your wife get fucked?" Ricky asked, confused.

Tom nodded his head and said, "Yeah, but I wanted it to be by a black man, and so did she. She showed me your picture on the Internet, and we both decided on getting in contact with you," Tom said solemnly. Ricky stood there shaking his head in total disbelief.

"Please, Ricky. He's harmless. All he wants to do is watch," Victoria pleaded.

"You didn't say anything about somebody watching me fuck you, Victoria!"

"I'm sorry, I didn't think you would do it," she confessed.

"You paid me $500 to fuck you; that's all you said to me," Ricky said, reaching down and picking up his boxers.

"Please, Ricky, don't leave," she begged.

"I'm outta here."

"Ricky, I'll pay you $1,500 if you stay!" Tom yelled out in desperation. Ricky stopped what he was doing and looked at both of them. He saw the serious expressions on their faces.

"Fifteen hundred, no strings attached, and all you gonna do is watch me fuck your wife?" Ricky asked.

"You got it," Tom said.

"Ricky, please . . . Please stay," Victoria pleaded softly.

Ricky tossed his pants and boxers back on the floor. He then looked at their smiling faces.

"You! Go stand over there!" Ricky instructed Tom.

Tom then walked over to the corner as Ricky climbed back on the bed with Victoria.

"Thank you for changing your mind," she said. Ricky turned her around on her stomach and started fucking her from behind. This time, he fucked her more aggressively. Victoria's screams and moans filled the room. While the orgasms flushed throughout her trembling naked body, her husband Tom stood in the corner smiling as he masturbated.

Chapter Twenty-Five

Confessions from the Heart

Sunday afternoon

When Ricky left Victoria and Tom's house, he drove straight home and went to sleep. He was tired, and his body was in need of rest. Before he got into his car and drove away, he made sure they had both gotten their money's worth. For them, it was a $2,000 investment with a great return. It turned out to be the best birthday present of Tom's entire life. He stood there watching and thoroughly enjoying himself as Ricky had his beautiful, sexy wife screaming and climbing up the walls of their bedroom. Ricky did things to Victoria that Tom never knew existed. That's why before Ricky left, Victoria and Tom promised to call him back very soon.

Once Ricky got back to his loft, he took a warm shower, and then went to bed. Early in the morning, he got dressed and drove over to his parents' house to see his daughter. Before Asia had left to go to church with her grandparents, she had told her father all about her wonderful day with India. After Asia and his parents drove off to church, Ricky called India on her cell phone and thanked her. Before he hung up the phone, he told her that she could now take out Asia whenever she wanted. India was excited beyond words. By giving his daughter away to someone else to look after, he had to have a lot of trust and faith in that person. No matter how long it would take her, India was determined to penetrate Ricky's impenetrable love shield.

Roscoe stood in the living room watching as Tori and Malinda walked out of the apartment carrying suitcases and bags. He stood there in total silence. But the anger in his eyes was clearly visible. When he tried to talk to Tori, she didn't want to hear it. Her mind was made up. The relationship was over. She told Roscoe that the most they could be was friends. She loved Roscoe for all that he had done for her. She wasn't in love with him or sexually satisfied by him. And Tori was fed up with settling for less.

Roscoe watched as the two women got into Tori's mother's Chevy minivan and drove away. He went back into his lonely, quiet room and slammed the door. He had to restrain himself from not pulling the 9 mm silencer from under his T-shirt and killing them both. The chance of one day getting Tori back is what had kept them alive today.

Roscoe sat down on the sofa and let the tears fall from his confused eyes. He could tell that Tori was hiding something from him, and he was determined to find out what it was. As anger clouded his thoughts, he sat back in tears. He knew that no lies last forever, and once the truth was revealed, someone would pay severely for all of his pain.

"Hello, Gloria, what's up?" Ricky said after checking the caller ID on his cell phone before he answered.

"You, as always. How's my young black lover doing?" she asked.

“Tired as hell!” he answered.

“Don’t burn yourself out, lover boy; then I won’t have no more use for you,” Gloria joked.

“I’ll be fine. Don’t I always come through?” Ricky teased back.

“Yes, you do, and I have no complaints at all. How’s the little one?”

“She’s fine. I went to see her this morning before she and my parents went to church,” Ricky said, looking at pictures of him and Asia up on the mantle.

“Gloria, can I ask you a question?”

“You always do, and I always answer truthfully.”

“Why don’t you and your husband have any children?” Ricky asked seriously. The question had caught Gloria completely off guard. For a few seconds, the phone went silent. “Gloria, you all right?” Ricky asked in a concerned voice.

“Yes, Ricky, I’m fine. You just hit me upside my head with a boulder I never saw coming,” she replied.

“I’m sorry, Gloria. You don’t have to answer that question.”

“No, Ricky, I enjoy our open, honest relationship. That’s what makes you stand out from most men. You’re a genuine, compassionate man who truly cares about the people in his life. Anyway, I can’t have children, Ricky. I’ve had that unfortunate problem for a long time now. My husband and I tried everything, but nothing worked. Adoption was out of the question. If I was gonna take care of a child, I wanted it to be my own.”

“Well, what’s the problem?”

“It’s hard to explain, Ricky. Many years ago, I had an affair on my husband. We had only been married a year. I got pregnant by my lover and had an abortion without my husband knowing. After the abortion, something just didn’t feel right. My mind and body weren’t the same.

Each time my husband got me pregnant, I lost the child. It felt like I was cursed by God. Not only did I commit adultery, I had murdered an unborn child, a child that never got a chance to cry, smile, to play, or live. On the day I had that abortion, I played the role of God. And by doing what I did, God cursed me to never have children and to never be satisfied with my marriage," Gloria said in a sad voice.

"Gloria, I'm sorry to hear that," Ricky said sincerely.

"Thank you, Ricky, and I believe you. Just never forget how blessed you are to have that beautiful daughter. If you ever find that true soul mate, do her right. Learn from the mistakes of others, and you will avoid many of your own."

For the next hour, Ricky and Gloria talked on the phone. Many times they would confide in each other about their problems. From the outside, they were two people who had it all: looks, money, and success, but inside them, both had a plethora of unwanted confusion.

Later that night

After India had hung up the phone with her new best friend Asia, she walked back over to the living-room table to where Nancy was sitting.

"Who was that?" Nancy said, counting a stack of hundred-dollar bills in her hand.

"A friend," India said, grabbing a handful of money from the table and helping her count.

"Male or female?"

"Does it matter, Mom?" India said in an irritated voice.

"Damn right it matters! You ain't been with a man since you came home from college, and I've been wondering—" Nancy began.

"Well, you can stop your worrying, Mother. All a woman can do for me is my hair, nails, and toes!" India said in a serious voice.

Nancy smiled. "Just wanted to make sure."

"I'll be fine, Mother, and besides, I have my eyes set on someone, and I know that he feels the same way about me."

"Then what's the problem?" Nancy said, putting a rubber band around the money stack. India stood up from her chair. She looked straight into her mother's eyes and said, "The problem is that there's another woman coming between us. For some strange reason, she won't let us have our happiness. One thing I learned about life is that when something is inevitable, there is nothing or no one that can stop it from happening," India said, turning and walking away.

"Mr. Orgasm! Mr. Orgasm! Mr. Orgasm!"

"What's my name?" Ricky asked as sweat covered his entire naked body.

"Mr. Orgasm! Mr. Orgasm!" Tori cried out as another orgasm exploded within her trembling body. Ricky was standing up in front of the mirror, with Tori's arms around his neck, and her legs wrapped around his waist. "I'm coming again! 'Mr. Orgasm,' you're making me come again!" Tori cried out in pure pleasure. "Oh my God!" she screamed slumping down on his shoulder.

Ricky walked over to the king-size bed and gently laid her down. Tori crawled up on a pillow and got in the fetal position. Her body was shaking and trembling with pleasure.

Ricky grabbed a dry towel from off the headboard and used it to wipe the wetness from between her thighs. He folded up the towel, then started wiping off her whole body.

He used another towel to wipe himself. When he climbed in bed with her, he cuddled her in his arms. He looked into her face and saw the look of a satisfied woman. He pulled the silk sheet over them both. It felt good on their skin.

"What you do to my body should be outlawed," she said softly.

"I can't do it without your participation, pretty," Ricky said, rubbing his hand across her body. "Rest up, pretty, 'cause we still got a long night ahead of us."

"Okay, just let me sleep for about an hour."

"How do you want to be awaken? With my warm tongue or my love stick?" he asked.

"Surprise me," she said as she dozed off.

Chapter Twenty-Six

Only God Knows

Monday afternoon

"Did you enjoy the CD I put together for you?" Twist said, riding in the passenger seat of Ricky's BMW.

"A classic!" Ricky said satisfied.

"Ricky, now I need a big favor from you," Twist said.

"Name it and you got it," Ricky replied, driving his car along the Schuylkill Expressway.

"I wanted to know if I could borrow your car Friday night."

"What's the special occasion?" Ricky asked, turning off the expressway and driving through the beautiful Fairmount Park.

"It's Kim's birthday. I just wanted to take her out to dinner and a movie in style."

"Yeah, no problem. You can borrow it. I have a date with the winner of the 'Mr. Orgasm' Number One Fan Contest, but I'll have a limo pick me up and my lucky date for a night out on the town," Ricky said with a smile.

"A limo?"

"Yeah, India put it altogether. The limo and dinner at a five-star restaurant for me and the lucky contest winner."

"What does the girl look like?" Twist asked.

"It's a blind date. I have to wait and see."

"Man, I know India don't like that. She can't hardly watch you give out yellow roses after you perform," Twist said.

"Well, the contest wasn't my idea. It was Nancy's. I think there were some other motives behind it," Ricky said seriously.

"Why do you think that?" Twist asked curiously.

"I think she set up the Number One Fan Contest because she knew I had thousands of female admirers."

"That's a good thing, ain't it?" Twist asked confused.

"Not if she's trying to turn her daughter off from me by putting her in charge of the contest. Letting India see all of my fans and go through all the e-mails they send me. The contest was just another one of Nancy's schemes to keep me and her daughter apart."

"I still don't understand why Nancy don't like you. And why wouldn't she want you and India to get together? It just seems like y'all two are perfect for each other. What's the real deal between you and Nancy?" Twist asked looking at Ricky while he continued to drive. Ricky pulled his car over to the side of the road. He turned down the radio and looked straight into Twist's face.

"Me and Nancy once had an affair."

"What! You and Nancy?" Twist asked in shock.

"Yeah; it was awhile ago. Right before her husband Richard was robbed and killed."

"Oh, this is before I got the DJ job there," Twist said.

"Yeah. Way before you arrived and many months before India graduated from Howard University and came back to Philly to help her mother run the club."

"You and Nancy had an affair?" Twist said again in total disbelief. "So what happened?"

"I broke it off. I just couldn't do it anymore! One minute I'm smiling in Richard's face, and the next minute I'm fucking his wife inside a suite at the Holiday Inn," Ricky said seriously.

"I just told Nancy that I couldn't do it anymore. She got angry with me, but I ain't care. My conscience was killing me."

"So that's why she treats you so bad. That's why she don't want you and India to be together," Twist said, putting two and two together.

"Yeah, but that ain't all, Twist," Ricky said.

"There's more?"

After a long sigh, Ricky said, "I think Nancy wanted me to kill her husband."

"What!" Twist shouted.

Ricky turned the radio off, sighed again, and said, "One night after making love, we were in bed talking. She asked me would I kill a man for $20,000."

"She did?"

"Yeah, and I had a feeling that she was talking about me killing her husband, Richard. I told her no, that I would never kill a man for money. After that night, I ended our affair. I knew she wouldn't like it, but I didn't care. I knew she wouldn't fire me from the club because I was the club's main attraction. She needed me. A few months after she asked me if I would kill a man for money, Richard was robbed and killed inside his office at the club. It was easy to put it all together at that point. Shit, she probably would've hung my ass up to dry for that murder."

"Do you think Nancy had something to do with it?" Twist asked.

"I honestly don't know, but that's a strange coincidence, wouldn't you say?" Ricky asked.

"Maybe Nancy got someone else to kill her husband since you wouldn't do it," Twist said.

"But she never asked me to kill her husband. She just asked would I kill a man for $20,000," Ricky said.

"Yeah, Ricky, but there has to be a reason for a woman to ask her young lover a question like that. A few months later, her husband ends up robbed and murdered? Something just ain't right," Twist said.

"When the police interviewed everyone at the club right after the murder, I didn't say nothing about what Nancy had said to me about killing a man for money."

"Why not?" Twist asked curiously.

"Because I didn't want to expose our secret affair, and plus, I didn't want my family, and especially my daughter, getting involved in it. So I told them that I didn't know anything, because it was best to keep myself out of it," Ricky answered.

"So that's why you avoid India and you hardly ever speak to her in front of her mother? You're protecting India from the truth," Twist said.

"Yeah, I guess you can say that. Plus, Nancy has threatened me and told me to stay away from her daughter, or *else*," Ricky said seriously.

"Or else what?" Twist said becoming angry.

"Or else I would end up like Richard!" Ricky muttered.

"She *told* you that?"

"Not in those exact words, but I knew what she meant."

"Man, this is crazy! Maybe Nancy told India to stay away. Why else would she have to sneak over to your parents' house to take out your daughter?" Twist asked.

"I don't know if she did or not, but, Twist, I'm not gonna lie to you. Every time I look into India's beautiful face, my heart feels like it's melting inside my chest. The first time I saw her, I was blown away by her beauty. I've had dreams about that woman! I've even made love to other women, closing my eyes and imagining them being her, just so it can help take my mind away from India!"

"Does it work?"

"Only until I see her beautiful face and that perfect smile again," Ricky said sadly.

"It's crazy that you can have almost any woman in the world—except the only woman that you truly want."

"Tell me about it," Ricky said, shaking his head. "There's another thing about India that I learned not too long ago," he said, pulling his car back on the highway.

"What's that?"

"I found out that India and Asia's mother, Cheryl's, birthdays are the same exact day. They are both Cancers born on June 28. Exactly six years apart, and that's the same age that Asia is now. And now India is involved in her life, and the two of them can't get enough of each other."

"Man, that's freaky!" Twist said. "Do you think that India is Cheryl reincarnated?"

"No, I wouldn't go that far, Twist," Ricky laughed. "But I will tell you this: when God takes away, he gives back to all of those who truly deserve it. He doesn't give us what we want, but what we need. He knows out hearts better than us. He knows our intentions, desires, and fears. He knows out wrongs and rights. He already has our soul mates prepared for each one of us. If all of these signs mean something, and India is the person that God wants in Asia's and my life, then it will happen, and nothing can stop it from happening. A lot of people on earth play God, but our God is a jealous God. None of them will go unpunished."

Ricky parked his car in front of the club; then he and Twist grabbed their bags and went inside. As soon as Ricky entered the club, India was right there to greet him. All he could do was shake his head.

Chapter Twenty-Seven

Killing Me Softly

Monday night

After the showstoppers had performed their twenty-minute exotic dance routine, each one of the dancers did their solo performance. Once again, Thunder, Neo, Flex, and Mr. Orgasm had all done their thing. Three hundred screaming female fans had gotten their money's worth. Ricky had come out on stage in a blue policeman's uniform, with all the accessories: badge, handcuffs, nightstick, hat, and dark shades. He slid across the stage on his knees, swung all around the pole, flipped, flexed, and even snaked his gorgeous body across the lighted stage. He performed his fifteen-minute erotic performance to Ginuwine's classic "Pony."

While Ricky was onstage doing his thing, DJ Twist was inside the DJ booth mixing and scratching the song throughout Ricky's entire solo performance. After Ricky tossed all his clothes and accessories into the boisterous crowd, he jumped off the stage and into a large crowd of swarming fans. India was standing on the balcony enjoying Ricky's entire show. But when she saw Ricky walk through the crowd and give an attractive-looking Puerto Rican woman one of his signature yellow roses, India had to force herself to control the tears that welled up in her eyes.

A few feet away, Nancy was watching India's every move with a big smile plastered on her face.

After Ricky and the beautiful Spanish female walked upstairs into one of the private, cozy, chitchat rooms, India eased out the side door when no one was looking. She climbed into her Range Rover, put her head down, and finally released the tears of sadness and pain from the confines of her eyes.

Roscoe and Damon sat inside the Escalade watching as the swarm of excited women started exiting the club. Cars and trucks were lined up and down the street, while music and marijuana flooded the air. When Roscoe spotted Tori and Malinda walking out of the club, he quickly got out of his truck and approached them. Both women were looking good, each dressed in the latest designer fashions: Dolce & Gabbana, Fendi, and Louis Vuitton.

"Tori, you got a minute?" Roscoe asked, looking into her beautiful light-skinned face.

"Roscoe, please don't start. I told you already that if you still would like to stay friends, then that's fine, but the relationship is over. Now, I don't want to fight with you, and I'm telling you this, not to hurt your feelings. I just made my decision, and I've decided to move on," she said seriously.

"So just like that? You saying fuck me, huh? After all I done for you!" he said angrily.

"She's not saying fuck you, Roscoe—" Malinda started to say.

"Bitch, shut the fuck up! I ain't talking to you, whore!" Roscoe yelled angrily. Tori saw the rage in Roscoe's eyes and just shook her head.

"I don't believe I was actually going to marry you! Now I see that women ain't nothing but bitches and whores to you. You disgust me, Roscoe!" Tori said walking over to her mother's parked car. Roscoe followed behind her and grabbed her arm. She pulled away and said, "So, now you grabbing on me, huh? First you call me a bitch in the apartment, and now you're calling Malinda a bitch and a whore, and pulling on my damn arm like some crazy-ass psycho," Tori said, upset.

"I just came over to talk to you, that all."

"What do we have to talk about, Roscoe? It's over! And why would you want to marry a bitch anyway?" she said opening the car door. She popped the lock and Malinda opened up the passenger door and got inside.

"Roscoe, stop making this shit worse than it is! I will always love you, but having love and being in love are two different things. Just like love and infatuation. I ended this relationship not only for myself, but for your own good as well. I was just tired of living a lie," Tori said as the tears welled up in her eyes.

"So you played me? Three and a half years you were just playing me like a sucka! Spending all my money and living the good life for free," he said vehemently.

"No, I was fucking you whenever you wanted sex, sucking your dick, cleaning up behind you, ironing your clothes, and everything else you needed from me. So don't even go there!" Tori retorted.

"So a nigga ain't got nothing to do with you breaking up with me?" he questioned.

"Is that all you think about is niggas? Did I ever ask you about your cell phone blowing up all throughout the night, or you coming and going whenever you pleased?"

"You still ain't answered me!" Roscoe said, seeing how she avoided the question.

"I told you already, and I'm not saying it again. No! Ain't no nigga got nothing to do with us breaking up!" Tori said as she angrily got into the car and slammed the door.

She started the car up and sped off down the street, leaving Roscoe standing there on the sidewalk. He looked around and saw all the people smiling, laughing, coming and going. When he walked back over to his truck, he saw Ricky getting inside of his BMW with a beautiful Puerto Rican woman. When Ricky drove past Roscoe's truck, he saw the painful look in Roscoe's eyes. From inside the club, Ricky had watched Roscoe and Tori arguing. He stood there at the window until Tori and Malinda had gotten in their car and drove off down the street.

After getting inside his truck, Roscoe turned to Damon and said, "That bitch cheated on me! I could see it in her lying eyes!"

"So what we gonna do?" Damon asked.

"First, I have to be 100 percent positive that I'm right. So what we gonna do on Wednesday night is go make a surprise visit to see Malinda," Roscoe said pulling off down the street.

"What if she won't talk?" Damon asked, rolling up the blunt of Haze.

"Oh, she'll talk. I *guarantee* that!" Roscoe said with an evil grin on his face.

Detective Hightower followed Flex to the Feather's Nest Motel in New Jersey. A day earlier, he had followed the secret lovers to the End of the Dove Motel that was also located in New Jersey. Even though the state of New Jersey was out of his jurisdiction, he was determined to get all of the information he could get on Nancy and Flex. Big Nook had given Hightower three of the tapes back with hours of recordings. Bobby had given him hours of audio footage on Flex. But Hightower still hadn't had any solid proof that Nancy played a part in her husband Richard's robbery and murder. So far, everything was all speculation.

Hightower watched as the skinny, white guy walked over to his car. He rolled down the window. The guy passed him a copy of the receipt for the room.

"She used her Platinum Visa credit card this time," the guy informed him. Hightower passed the skinny white man a $100 bill.

"Did you hear anything up there?" Hightower asked.

"The same as last month, Detective; moaning, grunting, and headboard banging. I had to call up in the room once to tell them to keep the noise down," the man said. "I don't think they take a break."

"Thanks, Smitty. I'm leaving now; call me tomorrow on my cell phone and let me know what time they clocked out," Hightower said.

"Sure will, Detective," Smitty said, putting the money in his pocket and walking back into the office.

Hightower backed his car out of the parking space and drove out of the parking lot. As he headed back to Philly, the thought of Nancy and Flex having sex in the motel room never left his mind.

After taking a nice warm shower, India dried herself off and walked into her cozy bedroom. She lotioned down her entire body, walked over to her wall stereo, and turned on the CD player. Crawling across her silk sheets, she lay there, inhaling the exotic aroma from the large scented candles she had placed all around her bedroom. Tears fell down from the corners of her eyes. Ricky had a lock on her heart that couldn't be broken, and it was killing her softly to not be able to do anything about it. She reached under her pillow and grabbed her Jack Rabbit vibrator. She had named her sex toy, "Mr. Orgasm," and began massaging her clit. With both eyes tightly shut, she let her wonderful sex toy do what it did best. India Arie's classic song, "Ready for Love," flowed out of the speakers.

The combination of touching, smelling, and hearing was her aphrodisiac. As the powerful orgasm swept throughout her trembling body, she lay there in the tranquility of her cozy bedroom, yearning, craving, lusting, and crying.

Chapter Twenty-Eight

The Scent of a Woman

Thursday evening

After Ricky and Thunder left the gym, Ricky got a call on his cell phone from Victoria. When he drove over to see her, she and her husband Tom were both smiling and waiting for him. One hour later, Ricky left the strange couple, sexually drained, and thousands of dollars richer. He drove over to his parents' house and enjoyed some quality time with Asia. All she talked about was her new best friend India and how India would call her every day to check up on her. While at his parents' house, Ricky enjoyed a delicious soul food meal with the whole family.

Afterward, he and Nicole walked outside and had a brief conversation. Nicole told Ricky about the B+ grade that Victoria had given her in psychology class. It was the first passing grade that she had received in the class.

After Ricky left the house, he drove over to the Executive Suites apartments on City Line Avenue, to go see his friend Carmen. When he got there, Carmen had surprised Ricky with a new pair of black alligator shoes, matching belt, and a cream-colored Versace mock neck sweater. They ordered a large Domino's pizza and sat on the sofa and watched a movie on Netflix. When Ricky finally left the apartment, Carmen's satisfied naked body was peacefully sleeping under her silk Gucci sheets.

When Ricky got home, he took a long, soothing, hot shower. After drying himself off, he put on his black Polo robe and slippers, then went into the cozy living room. He turned on his music and lay across the soft leather sofa. Once again, he thought about the cloudy direction of his young life. He couldn't help but think about India . . . beautiful India, his daughter's new best friend and role model. When the song "For you" by Kenny Lattimore flowed out of the speaker, Ricky smiled to himself. In the tranquility of his elegant home, he lay back thinking to himself while enjoying the music. The ringing of his cell phone interrupted his peaceful mood. For a second, he thought about not answering it; then, he changed his mind and picked it up.

"Hello," he said softly.

"Hi, Ricky, it's me, Tori."

"Hey, pretty. Tomorrow I'm going by your mother's house and dropping off that $1,000," he said.

"Ricky, you don't have to do that for me. I'll just wait," she said.

"Tori, I told you that I don't mind giving you the money to move into a new apartment. I know you don't want to be at your mother's house."

"But you don't have to do it."

"I want to do it. You're my new friend, and I really enjoy our times together, and besides, what are friends for?"

"Are you this way with all your female friends?" she asked.

"I try to be. Like I told you before, I have a lot of female associates who I care for, and who feel the same way about me. Sex is only a part of who I am and what I stand for. A lot of men are good in bed but lack everything else. Many men are good with everything else and lack in bed. I try to balance myself out. I try to be great in all aspects. The physical and sexual don't last forever, but respect, real friendships, and true love never fades," he explained.

"I believe you came into my life for a reason, and it has nothing to do with sex," Tori said. "If I ever do get married, I now know the kind of man that I'm looking for."

"I'm glad to be of some service," he laughed.

"So what are you doing right now?" she said, changing the subject.

"Lying back on the sofa enjoying my music."

"Do you mind having some company for a few hours?" she asked seductively.

"How soon can you get over here?"

"Walk to your front door."

Ricky got up from off the sofa and walked over to the door. When he opened it, Tori was standing by her mother's car. She was dressed in a long, black mink coat and a pair of strapped 3-inch heels. She stood there smiling, holding the cell phone to her ear. Ricky smiled and invited her inside the loft. She walked inside and shut the door behind her.

"You're pretty bold," he said, sitting down on the arm of the sofa.

"I didn't know if you had company or not. I just figured you didn't when you kept talking to me on the phone. But I promise you that I won't make this a habit," she said softly.

Ricky smiled. He actually liked her surprise visit.

"Well, since you're here now, let's sit back on the sofa and enjoy some good romantic R&B music," he suggested.

"Fine with me," Tori said, unbuttoning her mink coat and letting it slide down her shoulders and onto the carpeted floor. Ricky stared as Tori stood there in a red and black Victoria's Secret lingerie set. She walked over and joined him on the sofa. Her body was smelling good. Tori cuddled up under his arms. When Ricky's cell phone started ringing, he looked at the caller ID. It was the twins, Teri and Keri, from Trenton, New Jersey. He didn't answer.

"One of your friends?" she asked.

"No. Two," Ricky said, rubbing his hands across her arms and shoulders.

"Does this mean tonight I'ma have to make up for both of them?" she asked flirtatiously.

"Maybe," Ricky laughed softly. "But how about for now, we just lie back and enjoy this wonderful soul music?"

"Fine with me." As the smooth, soulful music filled the living room, they cuddled in each other's arms. Tori sat there enjoying his sensual touch on her skin, while Ricky sat back, enjoying the scent of the beautiful woman in his arms.

Chapter Twenty-Nine

No Lie Lasts Forever

Wednesday afternoon

After Ricky woke up in the morning, he took a quick, warm shower and left the loft to go pick up Asia for school. After he dropped her off, he went to the bank to deposit some money. Then he drove over to the gym and worked out with his friends Thunder and Neo for an hour. While Ricky was on his way back home, he got a call from the attractive Puerto Rican woman that he had met at the club on Monday night. Her name was Sophia. She asked him if he could swing by her job to see her. Sophia was the assistant manager at the Marriott Hotel in Center City, Philadelphia.

When Ricky walked through the Marriott's sliding glass door, Sophia spotted him right away. Tall, dark, and handsome. Bald with a goatee. Beautiful smile and sexy body. The perfect man, Sophia thought, as she approached him. They gave each other a hug, then walked into the elegant, spacious lobby. As they started hugging again, Sophia slipped a keycard inside his pocket.

"Room 312. It's empty. I'll be up there in one minute. That's when my lunch break starts, and I have a whole hour," she whispered in his ear. Ricky smiled, but before he released his hug on Sophia, he noticed a familiar face walking through the lobby.

"Don't move!" Ricky whispered in her ear.

"What's wrong?" she asked, tightening her grip around his waist.

"I see somebody I know," he said, walking Sophia over to a secluded area. When Ricky released his hug, they both stood there watching Nancy walk through the lobby and straight out the large glass doors.

"That's Mrs. Robinson, you know, the owner of Club Chances. She's a regular here," Sophia said. "She's here at least once a week, sometimes twice. Every time she comes, she meets up with that dancer you work with," Sophia said.

"What dancer? There's nineteen other exotic dancers at the club," Ricky said.

"The real cute one . . . Tall, light skinned, curly hair. The one who always dances before you," Sophia said.

"Flex?" Ricky said in shock.

"Yeah, that's his name," Sophia said.

"Do you know how long they've been meeting here?" Ricky asked.

"For a while now, at least seven or eight months," Sophia replied.

"What! Are you sure?" he asked, surprised.

"I'm the hotel's assistant manager. There's not too much I don't know that goes on here at the Marriott. There goes the guy right there," Sophia said pointing at Flex as he got off the elevator and rushed through the lobby. Ricky and Sophia both watched as Flex walked out the glass doors.

"Damn. I don't believe it!" Ricky said, standing there shaking his head. Ricky didn't *want* to believe it, but something inside of him was telling him that Nancy and Flex were behind her husband's murder.

"Room 312, right?" he said.

"Right. I'll be up there after I sign out for lunch," Sophia said as she walked away.

When the school bell rang, all the students stood up with their books and started walking out of the crowded classroom. Before Nicole left the classroom, Victoria called her name.

"Nicole, do you have a second?" Victoria asked, sitting down at her desk.

"Yes, Mrs. Langston, what is it?" Nicole said as she approached the teacher's desk.

"You did well today in class. I'm very proud of you," Victoria said.

"Thank you, Mrs. Langston. Psychology is hard, but I'm not gonna give up so easy," Nicole told her.

"Well, I just wanted to tell you that I appreciate what you did for me. Your brother Ricky is a wonderful man," Victoria said blushing.

"Yeah, I heard," Nicole said.

"Well, I just wanted to tell you to keep up the good work too. And if there is anything I can do to help you, don't be afraid to ask."

"Thank you, Mrs. Langston. I'll definitely hold you to that," Nicole said with a smile. "See you tomorrow, and I'll make sure I put another good word in to Ricky. Bye," Nicole said, walking out of the classroom. While Victoria sat in her chair daydreaming about the sex she had with Ricky, Nicole was walking down the crowded hallway.

Damn. Ricky must've rocked her world, Nicole thought to herself.

***

India stood by the window watching her mother park her Mercedes and rush from the car. When she walked into the club, India was standing there waiting for her.

"Mom, where have you been all morning? I had to open up, order the beverages for the bar, set the reservations for VIP tonight, and let all the workers and dancers in," India said, in a frustrated tone.

"That's your job when I ain't around. I had a meeting at the bank this morning, and then I had a very important run to make after the meeting at the bank was over," Nancy said, walking through the club. "Is everything ready for Ricky's blind date with the contest winner?" she asked.

"Yes, Mom, everything is set."

"Good. Since the contest was a success, I'm thinking about a contest for all the exotic dancers, since they all have their own group of fans. The contest is helping promote the club."

While Nancy and India were talking, Flex walked through the door.

"Hi, Mrs. Robinson, hi, India," he said, walking back toward the stage.

"Hi, Flex," they said in unison.

"I'll talk to you later. Tell Nook to meet me in my office," Nancy said, walking into her office and shutting the door. When Big Nook walked out of the men's room, India told him that her mother wanted to see him inside her office. Then she walked over to the empty table where her laptop computer was. Thirty minutes later, Ricky and Twist walked into the club.

Ricky sat down in the empty chair beside India and said, "What have you done to my little sweetheart?"

"Why? What's wrong?" India asked concerned.

"All she ever talks about now is her new best friend, India."

"I showed her love," India said.

Later that night

Ricky stood on the edge of the stage looking out at all the cheering female fans. His dark, muscular physique was covered in running sweat. While DJ Twist had the music blasting from the speakers, women in the boisterous crowd were filling the stage with money and panties. Ricky had turned the place out! The women were clapping and screaming out his name.

Ricky strolled across the stage looking for that lucky someone to give his special yellow rose to. Some women in the crowd were begging to be that special female he would take into one of the empty chitchat rooms. The large crowd was filled with familiar faces, and all eyes were on the famous "Mr. Orgasm." An attractive, slim, dark-skinned woman standing in the middle of the crowd caught his eye. Ricky jumped off the stage and danced his way through the crowd. He stopped midway in the crowd and started grinding on a heavyset, brown-skinned woman. The excited woman grabbed his dick from behind. Ricky just smiled as the horny, heavyset woman got her feel on. Other women were pulling on his arms and squeezing his ass.

After Ricky finally made it through the crowd, he passed the beautiful brown-skinned female the yellow rose and whispered in her ear. Her smooth chocolate face lit up with a big smile. Ricky turned around and danced his way back through the crowd. Once again, the women pulled on his arms, grabbed his dick, and squeezed his ass. When Ricky finally made it to the private chitchat room located on the second floor, his chocolate kiss was already standing there eagerly waiting for him.

Standing in a secluded area in the club, India had to hold back the tears. When she eased out the side door and got inside her Range Rover, she couldn't suppress the tears any longer.

When Roscoe and Damon watched all the women starting to pour out of the club, Roscoe started up his truck and sped off down the street.

"She'll be home in about twenty minutes," Roscoe said, driving through the red light.

After Ricky got dressed, he and his new friend walked out the side door and over to his parked car. Like a gentleman, he walked around to the passenger side and opened the door for her. When she climbed inside and shut the door, the woman leaned over and unlocked his door for him. Ricky got inside and started up his car. The engine to the BMW purred to life as the electronic dashboard lit up. Before Ricky pulled off, he saw India staring at him from inside the window. He could see the sadness in her watery eyes. Sighing, Ricky had to force himself to turn away. He knew that it was painful for India to see him leave with another woman. But what India didn't know was that it was just as hard for him.

Ricky turned to the beautiful female and said, "Ready?"

"I been ready!" she replied smiling, as he slowly pulled off.

Roscoe made sure that he parked his truck around the corner from Malinda's apartment. He and Damon was hiding behind a row of manicured bushes right outside of her apartment. They patiently watched as Tori pulled up in her mother's car and double-parked.

A few minutes later, Malinda got out of the car. She watched as Tori drove off. Roscoe and Damon were both dressed in all-black: sweatshirts, jeans, gloves, ski mask, and Tims.

As soon as Malinda walked up to her front door, they quickly jumped out and grabbed her. Roscoe held her arms while Damon punched her in the face as hard as he could. The hard blow knocked her unconscious. Then Damon used her door key to open the door, and they dragged her slumped body inside the empty apartment. They laid Malinda's body on the sofa. Damon shut the front door and rushed into the kitchen to get a glass of water. When he walked back into the living room, he threw the cold water in Malinda's face. She started slowly waking up. When she had finally regained consciousness, Roscoe and Damon were standing in front of her with pointed guns. Roscoe reached out and grabbed Malinda by the neck. A terrified look registered in her eyes.

"Bitch, what the fuck is going?" he said angrily. "What the hell is going on with Tori?"

"Roscoe, please! I don't know what you're talking about," Malinda said as tears sprang to her eyes.

"Bitch, you wanna play games?" he said, jamming the loaded gun between her eyes.

"Please don't kill me!" Malinda begged.

"Bitch, I'ma ask you just one more time. What the fuck is going on with Tori?"

Malinda saw the look of pure evil in his eyes. She trembled with fear.

"'Mr. Orgasm!' Tori and 'Mr. Orgasm' had sex last week at the club in one of those small private rooms," Malinda cried out.

"What!" Roscoe shouted.

"Tori met him back at his house one night and . . . and . . ."

"And *what,* bitch?" Roscoe said heated.

"And he turned her out! After being with him, she told me that she didn't want to be with you anymore," Malinda muttered.

Roscoe slapped Malinda with his gun. She fell back on the sofa with her hands covering her bloody mouth.

"Please, Roscoe! Please. I told you what you wanted to know! Please don't kill me!"

"Bitch, just like your adulterous-ass girlfriend; you're nothing but another whore who chase after money and sex!" Roscoe shouted angrily. The two men both stood over Malinda and pointed their guns. Before she could scream out for help, bullets riddled her body. They shot Malinda nine times in the face and chest. When they got back in the truck, Roscoe drove off down the dark street.

"As soon as I see that nigga Ricky, I'ma kill 'im! I put that on my unborn kids! And the same goes for that no-good whore Tori!" Roscoe said as a tear fell from the corner of his eye.

Chapter Thirty

The Consequences of Sin

Thursday

When Tori received the early-morning disturbing phone call from Malinda's landlord, her painful scream filled the entire house. Malinda's shot-up body was discovered when the landlord came by to fix the bathroom sink. After seeing Malinda's bloody, almost unrecognizable corpse lying on the sofa, the landlord immediately called 911. He then called Tori, who was listed as Malinda's emergency contact. Malinda's body was immediately taken to the Philadelphia Medical Examiner's office. The slaying was broadcast all over the TV news and radio. The police had no clues or witnesses. And the neighbors had told the detectives that no gunshots were heard. Tori was now scared for her life. Something deep inside of her was telling her that Roscoe, her ex-fiancé, was the person behind this brutal murder. Killing Malinda was the warning to let her know that she was next to die.

With the money that Ricky gave her, Tori left her mother's house and used it to check in at a motel. She took a week's worth of clothes and her cell phone with her. When she got to the motel, Tori called her job and asked her boss for an emergency leave of absence. Her boss at the hospital, who had learned about the tragic murder from watching the news, told Tori to take as much time as she needed. Inside her motel room, Tori let the tears of pain, sorrow, and loss drip from her terrified face. At the same time, she had never been more scared in her life.

Roscoe and Damon had been driving all around West and Southwest Philadelphia searching for Ricky. When they met Flex at the club and asked him if he saw Ricky around, Flex told them that he hadn't seen him and wasn't expecting to until the next strip show on Monday night.

They asked Flex some more questions about Ricky, but he didn't have any more info to give them.

"When you see that nigga, call me ASAP!" Roscoe told Flex before driving off.

When Roscoe drove by Tori's mother's house, the elderly woman told him that Tori had left the house with her suitcase and got into a cab. Roscoe knew that Tori was now running for her life.

With their loaded 9 mm Berettas under their shirts and a loaded AK-47 lying on the back floor of the stolen car, Roscoe and Damon continued to drive around on their murderous hunt. With the look of pain on their faces and revenge inside their hearts, Roscoe and Damon were determined to track down Ricky and Tori. They both had crossed a dangerous line. The power of lust, sex, and infatuation had been the cause. While Tori was inside of a North Philly motel, scared for her life, Ricky had no idea that he was now a wanted man. As the two men continued to drive around looking for their next two victims, no words were spoken, because both men knew that Malinda's brutal murder was just the beginning.

Friday

Ricky got out of his BMW and walked around the driver's side to where Twist was seated. Twist rolled down the window and shook Ricky's hand.

"Take care of my baby," Ricky said.

"Don't worry, Ricky. I got you, homeboy. I'm just gonna hang out with my girl for her birthday and show off a little," Twist said with a smile. "I'll call you in the morning. Enjoy your blind date."

"Hopefully, I will," Ricky said walking toward his loft. Ricky stood there and watched as Twist drove off down the dark street. When he disappeared, Ricky went into his loft to get himself ready for his blind date with the contest winner.

After taking a hot shower, he dried himself off, lotioned down his muscular body, and put on his clothes. Ricky was impeccably dressed, looking sharp as a blade. He wore a black Polo blazer, a cream-colored Versace mock neck, black Polo slacks, and a pair of black Gucci loafers. His head was freshly shaved, and his goatee was nicely shaped up. The Polo fragrance covered his body. The iced-out Rolex covered his wrist, and the 1-carat diamond earring lit up his left ear.

It was 7:35. Ricky was expecting the limo to come pick him up at 8:00. That was the time that India had told him it would be there. He sat on the sofa listening to the music as he waited. A song by Norah Jones flowed out of the speakers. Ricky got lost in her beautiful voice, but soon, the sound of a loud horn brought him out of his peaceful zone.

He turned off the music and dimmed all the lights. When he walked out the front door, an all-black stretch Mercedes-Benz limousine was parked in front of his loft. After locking his door, Ricky walked over to the limo, opened the back door, and slid inside. The driver rolled down the tinted separation glass and said, "Hi, Mr. Johnson. My name is Charlie. I'm your driver for the evening. I'll be taking you to meet your companion for the evening. She's currently waiting as we speak. If there's anything you need, just pick up the phone and call me up front. I was told not to disturb you for the rest of the evening. There's champagne in the bar and a TV if you get bored. I hope you enjoy yourself tonight," he said, turning back around and pressing a button that rolled up the thick, tinted separation glass. Ricky reached over and turned on the radio to WDAS, a popular Philadelphia radio station which was playing classic R&B songs.

"If Only You Knew" by Philly's own Patti LaBelle, flowed smoothly from out of the sound system. Ricky relaxed in the comfortable leather seat and started humming the melody. The song brought back so many wonderful memories. As the limo cruised through the dark Philly streets, he closed his eyes and once again, let himself get lost in the music.

Chapter Thirty-One

The Point of No Return

Half an hour later

The limo pulled up and stopped at a secluded area near Penn's Landing. Charlie rolled down the tinted separation glass and said, "This is where your date asked me to come pick her up. She'll be wearing all-black." Then he rolled the window up.

Ricky opened the door and stepped outside of the car. He stood there looking all around. There was a nice cool breeze coming from the calm Delaware River. A full moon was high up in the sky, surrounded by bright shining stars. The temperature was in the mid-sixties, perfect for a pleasant fall night.

He turned around and noticed a woman dressed in black slowly walking toward him. Nervousness filled his body. He couldn't see her face, but he could see that she was tall and slim. The closer she got, the more he recognized her face.

When India finally approached him, Ricky stood there with surprise written all over his countenance. India looked stunning; her face, hair, and that perfect smile. She was dressed in a black satin-trimmed wrap dress by Vera Wang. On her pedicured feet was a pair of black Prada stiletto boots. Ricky stood there in total silence.

India stood there staring into his shocked brown eyes while tears fell from the corner of hers.

"I've been waiting for this moment with you from the very first time I ever saw you. This time, I'm not gonna let you run away." India grabbed his hands and continued to look into his eyes. "I'm tired of crying for your attention, yearning and craving your love. Thinking about you all day, every day. Touching myself at night, wishing that it was you instead; chasing you and seeing you running away. I love you, Ricky. I love you, and I'm not afraid to say it because this is how I feel. I love your daughter. I love everything about you. I don't care what happened in your past or what's going on between you and my mother. I will not let you continue to run away from me. I will not go another minute from this moment on, without you being a part of my life," India cried out.

Ricky looked into her serious, watery eyes and started wiping her tears.

"Ricky, if you feel what I feel, just tell me. Please, Ricky, I gotta know," she said desperately.

Slowly, Ricky said, "India, in all my life, I have only told one woman that I love her, and that was Asia's mother, Cheryl. Tonight, I can honestly look into your eyes and say that what I feel for you is a feeling that I've never known before. Yes, India, I do love you," Ricky professed as they embraced each other and started kissing passionately. For five undisturbed minutes, they kissed without separating for a break. Both of them were burning with desire and passion. They were more turned on than they had ever been in their lives.

They got into the limo and closed the door. Charlie rolled down the window and said, "Where to?"

"Back to his place," India said as their tongues got reacquainted.

About twenty minutes later, the limo pulled up in front of Ricky's private loft. After Ricky shut the door, they were at each other like two wild animals in heat, snatching and tearing off each other's clothes. Their bodies couldn't be apart another moment. Cupid had called, and both their ears had heard his loud voice.

Ricky picked up India's naked body and carried her into his mirrored-covered bedroom. He placed her on the bed and quickly joined her. Ricky climbed onto her body, and once again, they started kissing passionately, their hearts beating as one.

"Make love to me, Ricky. Make love to me now!" India cried out.

In one smooth motion, Ricky slid his hard, long dick into India's wet and silky paradise. She moaned out in pleasure as she reached her arms around and cupped Ricky's ass while he stroked in and out of her. She matched him stroke for stroke, meeting his with every thrust.

"Oh yes! Make love to me good," India moaned softly. Ricky licked around her neck and earlobes. The feeling was so good that he could feel himself coming inside of her. He hadn't had sex without a condom since Cheryl.

"Oh, I'm coming!" Ricky grunted, exploding deep inside of her.

"Let it all out, baby! Keep making love to me!" India moaned as she pulled Ricky's trembling naked body closer to hers. Ricky was so turned on that his dick was still rock hard. He put India's legs up on his shoulders and started stroking inside of her with all the force in his body.

"Oh! Ahh! Ohh! Oh! Ricky, I'm com-coming! I'm coming, baby!" India cried out. The powerful orgasm swept through her trembling body as sweat dripped from both of them.

"Oh, Ricky! Ohh, Ricky, I love you! I'm-I'm coming again!" India screamed out in pure pleasure.

They were both so turned on that neither one of them wanted to stop. Both of their bodies had been taken over by a sexual force that wouldn't be denied—a force of lust, passion, and love.

When Ricky lay on his back, India straddled herself on top of him and slid his still hard dick into her throbbing wetness. They melted in each other's arms. They grunted and moaned out each other's names.

Ricky lay back impressed with India's flexibility. She was riding him like a born pro, as if his dick was made perfectly for her. India rode Ricky until his toes curled, and he came inside of her wet pussy again. She could feel his thick love cream filling up her insides. She sucked on his lower lip and kept on riding away.

"Oh, I'm coming again!" India screamed, riding him harder and faster. "Oh, Ricky . . . Oh . . . Oh, Ricky! I'm having an orgasm!" India said slumping down on his sweaty chest.

Ricky turned her body around and crawled down between her thighs. While India lay back trembling, he teased her clit with his warm tongue. He did the alphabet trick with his tongue, starting from A–Z. Then he did the same trick in reverse from Z–A.

"Oh yes! Oh yes!" India said as the wonderful feeling made her come once again.

Ricky was far from done with her. It was now time for him to perform his famous triorgasm trick on her. First, he started stimulating her clit. Then he slowly moved his warm, wet tongue to her vagina for a few minutes, then slowly back to the clit. When he felt India reaching her peak, he used two of his long fingers to stimulate her G-spot and anus at the same time. The pleasing sensation started heightening sensitivity all throughout her trembling body, giving India's satisfied body an earth-shattering orgasm.

"Oh! Oh! Ahhh! My God! Ricky! Ricky! I'm having another orgasm!" India cried out in ecstasy. Ricky crawled up on her naked body and slide his dick back inside of her. India looked into his eyes and said, "Tell me you're all mine, Ricky! Tell me!" she cried as he stroked in and out of her.

After a long passionate kiss, Ricky looked into her serious eyes and said, "From this moment on, I'm all yours, India!" The words were like music to her ears.

Twist and his attractive young girlfriend never noticed the stolen dark green Buick Regal following close behind them. For four blocks the car was close on their tail. Twist and his girlfriend Kim were inside the BMW enjoying music from the radio. When Twist pulled into the parking lot of the AMC movie theater on Delaware Avenue, the Buick quickly pulled up and blocked them off. Suddenly, two masked men jumped from out of the car. One of the men was carrying a Russian AK-47 machine gun, and the other had two loaded 9 mm Berettas in his hands.

Twist and his beautiful girlfriend didn't have a chance. The sounds of nonstop shooting filled the dark sky. It sound like the Fourth of July was happening in the middle of September. Twist and his girlfriend died instantly on her birthday. Their mangled bodies slumped down inside the bullet-riddled BMW. The two shooters quickly got back into the stolen car and sped off through the parking lot. When the police finally arrived on the scene, they saw the brutal massacre of the young teenagers. The vicious assassins were already long gone.

After ditching the stolen car, Roscoe and Damon got back inside the Escalade. Damon rolled up another Haze-filled blunt and lit it up. They passed it back and forth blowing the thick smoke into the air. There were no words spoken. No grief for taking two lives. Murder was easy for them. The consequence of sin was a penalty that every sinner must one day face.

Chapter Thirty-Two

Soul Mates

Saturday morning

Ricky and India made love all night long, literally. Together, their bodies experimented with every sexual position in the book: missionary, doggie style, reverse cowgirl, on top, sideways, standing, sitting, oral, anal, and 69. Now they lay in bed staring into each other's satisfied eyes.

"I'm not leaving you, Ricky. It's all about us now," India said walking her fingers up and down his arm. "I want you to tell me everything, and I promise I won't hold anything against you," she said in a serious voice.

Ricky sat up on the bed and said, "I have a lot of female friends, and that's all they've been—friends. To be honest, I kept it that way because a part of me was holding out for you, but after today, I will call each one of them and tell them that I can no longer be their private dancer. I want my daughter to have a real family, and I want it to start today, with you and me." After Ricky revealed everything about everyone, he said, "I have something else that I really need to tell you."

"Is it about the affair you had with my mother?"

"What? How did you . . . know?" he asked, shocked.

India sat up beside him. She reached out and grabbed his hand.

"Before I graduated from college and came back to Philly to help my mother run the club, my father and I had a very long talk. He told me that he and my mother were no longer getting along, and he asked for a divorce. He also told me that he was almost positive that my mother was having a secret affair.

"After my father was robbed and murdered and I came back to help my mother, the first thing I noticed wrong was the way she would always treat you, how she would treat the number one dancer at the club like he was nothing. Almost every day, she had something bad to say about you. The first and only person that she told me to stay away from was you. Not pretty boy Flex or big boy Thunder or anyone else. Just you! Whenever you came around me, she chased you away. Many times she discussed the idea of switching your and Flex's dance positions.

"After a while, I started to put two and two together. One day, I said to myself, how can she not like a humble, honest, respectable man who loves his daughter and who's also responsible for the success of her own club? Something just wasn't right! Then there were so many other things that she did. Like the Number One Fan Contest, trying to make me jealous. That's when I finally figured that you were the one who must have ended the affair. That's why she can't stand you to this day."

Ricky just shook his head in total amazement. "Girl, you're good," he said with a smile. "India, the truth is, that your mother's and my affair only lasted a month, and I broke it off because of your father. I was tired of smiling in your father's face and then sleeping with his wife behind his back. The guilt was killing me. That's when I decided to end the affair with your mother. I knew that she would be upset with me, but I honestly didn't care anymore. I had made up my mind, and I was standing on my decision," Ricky said seriously.

"Is that all? It seems like you want to say more," India said.

"No, there's one more thing that turned me off completely from your mother."

"Just say it. I want you and me to be totally honest with each other from this moment on. I don't care what it is, Ricky. I believe we are soul mates, and together, we can get through anything that the devil puts in our way."

"Your mother asked me one day if I would kill a man for $20,000."

"What!" India shouted in disbelief.

"I told her no, and that was the last of our affair."

India reached out, and they gave each other a long, passionate hug. Tears fell from her eyes. Ricky looked into India's crying eyes and said, "We are two people with so many burdens, and now it's time to start pushing them all away."

After a sweet kiss, Ricky said, "I'll start telling my female friends that I've found my soul mate, and I will also tell your mother that I'm quitting my job at the club. My exotic dancing days are all over. Now, any show I perform will only be for you."

"Before you quit, I would really like for you to do just one more show," India said.

"Why's that?" Ricky asked curious.

"Because, you *owe* me," India said with a smile.

Ricky got out of bed, and India sat there watching as his fine, naked, Adonis black body walked out of the bedroom. Moments later, the smooth, melodic voice of Boyz II Men started flowing out of the speakers. India lay back smiling on the king-size bed. She rested her head on a large, soft pillow. Looking up at the ceiling, she saw her reflection staring back at her in the mirror.

While Ricky was inside the kitchen, he heard his cell phone ring. He thought about answering it, but then he decided not to. Whoever it was could wait, he thought.

His passionate night with India had been long overdue. He didn't want to be disturbed by anyone.

When he walked back into the bedroom, he had a breakfast tray in his hands. On the large tray was cheese eggs, turkey bacon, grits, toast, strawberry jelly, two glasses of orange juice, knives and spoons. He set the tray on the bed; then he joined his beautiful soul mate.

"So after you drain my entire body, you fill me back up, huh?" India said with a smile.

"I guess you can say that," Ricky smiled.

"Well, I'ma have to spend a whole lot of money on food shopping," India said with a smile.

"And why is that?"

"I have a lot of sexual energy in me. If I'm drained, then you will be too," India said laughing.

Chapter Thirty-Three

The Cries of Pain

Late Saturday night

Wrapped inside of India's loving arms, Ricky and India cried throughout the whole night. When Ricky found out about the brutal slaying of Twist and his girlfriend, Kim, he just couldn't believe it. After talking to Tori and learning about her girlfriend Malinda's murder, they both realized that Roscoe and Damon had to be the two culprits responsible for the three homicides. The loss of his young friend Twist gave Ricky a pain that couldn't be explained. It felt worse than a knife stabbing his crying heart. Ricky knew that the brutal slaying was intended for him and Tori, and not for Twist and Kim. It was something that he would have to live with forever. He knew that even though he hadn't committed the murders, he was just as responsible. Because of his actions, innocent people were now dead. Ricky told Nancy that he wouldn't show up at work until things settled down. He wanted to tell Nancy that he had quit, but he didn't because he had promised his new girlfriend, India, one last performance.

When Sunday morning came, Ricky started calling all of his female friends, telling them that he was no longer a single man. They all understood. Each one wished him well with his new relationship. The last three women that were left to tell were Carmen, Tori, and Gloria. For Ricky, because of the bond that he's shared with these three women, he felt that a phone call wouldn't suffice. These women had actually grown to be some of his best friends. It was important to him that he showed them the respect that a phone call or a text message just couldn't offer. As much as he'd been there for each of them, they had equally been there for him as well. At times when he was going through things and needed a listening ear, they'd been just that.

"Come on, you're going with me," Ricky said. He and India got into her Range Rover and headed for the Executive Suites on City Line Avenue. When Ricky pulled into the parking lot, Carmen was standing there waiting beside her car. Ricky parked beside her and got out. India remained seated in the passenger seat.

"So you finally found her, huh?" Carmen asked, smiling.

"Yeah. I'm sorry—"

"Don't be sorry. I'm happy for you," Carmen said cutting him off. "You're a very special man, Ricky, and I'm sure that she must be very special also or else you wouldn't have driven over here with her. That's the pretty girl who manages the club, I see," Carmen said looking over at India.

"Yeah. She's the one," Ricky said.

"I've seen the way that y'all two always looked at each other. I knew that it had to be something."

"So you noticed, huh?"

"Many times," Carmen said. "Love has been in both of y'all's eyes for a while."

"I want you to know that I'm still here for you, no matter what. Just because there will be no more sex between us doesn't mean that we still can't be friends," Ricky said seriously.

"Ricky, as much as I enjoyed the exciting sex, I love the genuine person you are. I'll always be your friend, and I know you'll always be mine. I want you to know that I'm really happy for you, and I appreciate all the wonderful memories that you left me with. What's your girlfriend's name?"

"Her name is India."

"Pretty," Carmen said, walking over to the passenger-side window. India rolled down the window.

"Hi," she said innocently.

"Hi, India. Ricky told me your name. I just wanted to tell you that you have a very special man, and I truly wish the best for y'all," Carmen said sincerely.

"Thank you so much," India said in a sweet voice.

Carmen walked back over to Ricky, and they embraced in a long, passionate hug. Before he got back inside the Range Rover, he said, "Before you marry Hardrock, I want you to *really* think about everything. You are a black queen, so please don't settle for less. Don't let sex or money control your decision, because neither one will last forever."

As Ricky got back into the SUV, Carmen stood there in tears. Then he and India slowly drove out of the parking lot.

Ricky's next stop was at a small motel on Roosevelt Boulevard. Tori was waiting out back when the red Range Rover pulled up and parked. Ricky got out and approached her. Her face showed fear and worry. They gave each other a warm hug. Before he said a word, Ricky went into his pocket and took out five new one hundred-dollar bills. He gave them to her.

"This is for you to stay here for a few more weeks until things settle down. If you run out or need more, just call me. I told you that I'm a true friend, and one thing that I will never do is abandon you," he said earnestly.

"Is that your new friend?" Tori asked.

"Yes. Her name is India, and she's my new and only woman," Ricky said. "I just wanted to tell you face-to-face. I didn't want to lie. We both know that neither Roscoe nor I am the right man for you, Tori. You deserve so much better, and neither one of us can give you that. Your relationship with Roscoe was based mainly on money and wants. Ours was strictly sexual. You need a man that will give you so much more. I'm not that man. I'm in love with that woman inside that truck, and I have been for a while. But if you ever need me, I'm just a call away, and that's my word. I'm truly sorry about your friend, but just know this: What comes around goes around. God don't like ugly."

"Thank you, Ricky. Thank you so much," Tori said, crying.

After a long hug, Tori cried as she watched Ricky and India back up the Range Rover and drove away.

Ricky called Thunder on his cell phone and told him to meet him back at his private loft. After he hung up, Ricky called Gloria and asked her if she could get away. She told Ricky that she was on her way over and would be at the loft in an hour.

When the luxurious Rolls-Royce Phantom pulled up and parked, Ricky, Thunder, and India were all standing outside. Gloria stepped out of the car looking like one of the models from *Vogue* magazine. From head to toe, she was dressed in Christian Dior—dress, heels, glasses, and jacket. When she looked over at the beautiful young woman wrapped inside of Ricky's arms, she already knew why he had called her. Ricky asked India and Thunder to wait while he walked over to Gloria. They gave each other a hug. Gloria took off her frames and said, "I see you have wonderful taste. She's very beautiful."

"So you know, huh?" Ricky said.

"The only thing that lasts forever is love, handsome," Gloria said in a soft, serious voice. "I felt it on the drive over here, and now seeing her and you together, it's obvious that the two of you are in love and belong together."

"I just wanted to keep my promise to you," Ricky said sincerely.

"I knew you would. I expected nothing less of you. So this is it, huh?" Gloria asked in a sad voice.

"Yes, I'm afraid, but I want you to know that I'll always be here for you, just not sexually. Everything you gave me I'm returning it all back," Ricky said.

"No, I won't accept it. Believe me when I tell you, handsome, you earned every bit of it," she countered.

"Well, I'll accept it all except the loft. I'm moving out in a few weeks and will be getting a house for me, Asia, and my new girlfriend," Ricky informed her.

After a long sigh, Gloria said, "You're one helluva man, Ricky, and being with you has taught me a lot about myself. I can look into your happy eyes and see that you've finally found your soul mate. Just make her proud and make sure you two set an example for other young couples. Lord knows the world needs more. I wish there were more men like you."

"My friend is over there. His name is Thunder, and I wanted to introduce you two," Ricky said smiling.

Gloria looked over at Thunder and smiled. Then she turned back to Ricky and said, "I see you know my taste."

"Tall, dark, and handsome, right?" he said smiling.

"Perfect," Gloria said looking back over at Thunder and eyeing him up and down. "Your friend is a big boy. I wonder if he's flexible," Gloria said flirtatiously.

"Well, you can find out for yourself. My girlfriend India and I have to go make an important run, and afterward, we're driving to Baltimore for a few days," Ricky informed her.

"What's in Baltimore?"

"Nothing. We just wanted to get out of the city for a few days, and I've never been there." Ricky called Thunder over to him and Gloria. When Thunder walked up, he and Gloria both stared into each other's lust-filled eyes.

"So your name's Thunder, huh?" she asked, flirting.

"That's what they call me," he quickly responded blushing.

"And why is that?" Gloria continued to flirt.

"Because everything I do, I do it hard like thunder! I make sure a person *feels* me," he said seriously.

Gloria could feel herself already getting wet. Just looking up at the large, black man had turned her on. Thunder wasn't as handsome as Ricky, but he wasn't ugly either. His huge body was a much-bigger version of Ricky's.

"I'll leave you two alone. Thunder has a key to the loft. Don't break nothing," Ricky said joking as he walked away. Gloria reached out and grabbed Thunder's huge hand.

"I can't promise you that," she told Ricky as she and Thunder walked toward the front door of the loft.

"Gloria, take it easy on him," Ricky said laughing as he and India got back into the Range Rover.

"I'm sorry, Ricky, but I can't promise you that either," she said with a smile.

After Gloria and Thunder walked into the loft and shut the door, Ricky slowly pulled off. They had one more stop to make; one that truly mattered.

Nancy's house.

Forty-five minutes later

Nancy was looking out of her bedroom window when she saw India's red Range Rover pull up in the driveway and park. She quickly ran out of her bedroom and down the stairs. Nancy hadn't seen or heard from India in two days. When she called her, India refused to answer her calls. India walked through the door and saw Nancy standing there with her hands on her hips.

"Where the hell have you been at?" she fumed.

"I've been fucking my man! The same thing you been creeping around doing with your lover Flex!" India shouted.

A shocked expression instantly came over Nancy's face.

"Don't you talk to me like that. I'm still your mother!" Nancy stated.

"You're nothing but a jealous whore who cheated on my father! I know everything! All about your and Ricky's affair and why you hate him so much. I also know about you and Flex creeping all around the city in different hotels."

"How . . . how . . . do you know that?" Nancy asked in shock.

"It doesn't matter. What matters now is you will no longer have any control of my life! You have always been a money-hungry, manipulating liar! Nothing hurts me more than calling you my mother! My father loved you with all of his heart, and all you ever cared about was his money! You slept with two different men who worked at the club. I hate you! I hate you for everything you stand for! I'm leaving this house! I don't want anything that reminds me of you! If you had anything to do with my father's murder, I hope you rot in hell!" India vented, screaming at her mother.

Nancy stood there in confused tears. Her whole body was trembling with sadness and pain.

"Save your phony tears. You're only sorry because I found out the truth about your deceitful ways! Now, I want you to see who I been fucking, and enjoying every single moment of it! The same man that I'm gonna one day marry and give lots of beautiful children to," India said opening the front door. Standing right there in the doorway was Ricky. Nancy almost fainted.

"You don't want us to love each other, because he wouldn't love you. The only thing that you and your money can't stop is true love! It was inevitable for us to connect and become one. We are soul mates, and that's something that you will never have as long as you live, because when you did have yours, you didn't appreciate him," India said.

"India, please. Please, India, I'm your mother. Give me a chance," Nancy cried out.

"Did you give my father a chance?"

The powerful words felt like a stab in the heart. Nancy fell down to her knees crying with her face to the floor.

"Mother, I do want to thank you for one thing. For showing me how *not* to be the woman *you* are," India said walking out the door and slamming it behind her.

Nancy remained on her knees in tears. She could hear India's truck starting up and driving away. Money, lust, power, and sex had always been her motivation, but none of them combined could cure her crying soul. Her daughter's harsh words had done more damage to Nancy than a knife or a gun. Now she sat weeping, filled with pain.

Chapter Thirty-Four

When the Tables Turn

Three days later, Wednesday afternoon

While Ricky and India were in Baltimore, they stayed at the luxurious Embassy Suites Hotel. Together, they shopped, dined out at fine Italian, Cajun restaurants, and enjoyed soul food. They saw a wonderful show at a local jazz club and visited the famous Baltimore Harbor, where they took in the lovely view and ate fresh crabs. In the daytime, they visited all of the famous Baltimore sights. At night, in the tranquility of their private suite, they made blissful, uninhibited love. They had such a wonderful time that they decided to stay for a few more days. While Ricky and India were in Baltimore loving their heavenly break from the rest of the world, in Philly, all hell was about to break loose.

When Flex walked into Club Chances, Big Nook and three of his men quickly grabbed him and threw him to the ground. Nancy was inside her office when she heard all the commotion going on inside the club. She ran out of the office and saw Flex handcuffed and being read his Miranda rights by Big Nook.

"Nook, what the hell is going on?" she yelled.

"Nancy, Flex is being arrested and charged with the distribution of drugs and selling an illegal substance to minors," Big Nook said as he lifted Flex off the ground and walked him outside.

Nancy followed the group of police officers out of the club. When she walked outside, police officers swarmed everywhere. Big Nook pushed Flex in the back of the police van and slammed the door. Then he walked over to Nancy and said, "I've been on an undercover investigation for quite a while now. I've gathered enough info on Flex that will put him away for thirty years."

"So, all you got on Flex is some drugs?" she questioned nervously.

"He can't discuss that with you, Mrs. Robinson, but I'm sure you'll be hearing from us very shortly," Detective Hightower said, walking up from behind her. When Nancy saw Hightower's face, her heart felt like it had dropped inside of her chest.

"Remember me?" he said, smiling.

How could she ever forget? Hightower was the detective that was assigned to her husband's murder case. Nancy stood there watching as all the police officers got back into their cars and vans and drove off. All the male dancers stood around watching in total disbelief.

"Everybody can go home. The club will not be open tonight. I'll notify each and every one of you when I plan on reopening," she said, rushing inside and going back into her office.

Flex was handcuffed to a table inside the 18th Police District interrogation room.

"I don't know shit! Get me a lawyer!" he shouted.

"You think this is a damn game, huh?" Hightower barked.

He walked over to the door and opened it. "Bobby, come in here," he said.

When freckle-faced, braces-wearing Bobby walked in the room with a smile on his face and his shiny police badge hanging around his neck, Flex's eyes almost popped out of his head.

"Okay, tough guy. Meet Officer Bobby Reynolds," Hightower said smiling.

"Oh shit," Flex said, slumping down in the chair.

"If you don't tell us everything we need to know, I'm gonna make sure the judge throws the book at you. Right now, Flex, with all the drugs, surveillance, and wire-tapped conversations we got on you, you're looking at a minimum of thirty years at a maximum state correctional facility," Hightower yelled. "We got you, pretty boy, and if you don't cooperate, the guys at the state pen will have your pretty ass bleeding for thirty, long years."

Flex sat there with a scared look on his face. When he looked over at freckle-faced Bobby, he just shook his head. There was only one way out of the situation he had put himself in.

"What do you want to know?" he said defeated.

"Everything! Nancy, Roscoe, and Damon. And if you lie to us, say good-bye to the deal we'll ask the prosecutor to give you. So, either tell us everything, Flex, or do thirty years. Period."

Four hours later, Flex had told Detective Hightower and the other interrogators everything he knew. He told them all about Nancy's plot to kill her husband Richard, and about the $20,000 cash that she paid him to do it. Flex told the detectives who had given him the gun to kill Richard and all about the drugs that he sold for Roscoe and Damon. What surprised the detectives the most, especially Big Nook, was when Flex told them all about

Nancy's murder plot to kill Ricky. Nancy had offered Flex $30,000 to kill the man who had broken her heart. She was willing to pay $10,000 more than she paid for the murder of her own husband.

Later that night, Nancy was arrested at the Philadelphia International Airport. She was charged with conspiracy to murder her husband, Richard. Her secret lover, Flex, snitched her out.

Friday afternoon

Roscoe and Damon were sitting inside the living room of Roscoe's apartment, smoking the Haze-filled blunt. On the large coffee table were nine handguns, 25,000 X-pills, and stacks of counterfeit money. Inside the box on the floor was the rest of the guns and ammo that they had killed Troy for. When the ATF, DEA, and FBI officers busted in through the front door, both men were completely caught off guard. Hightower had notified the feds about the two dangerous men, knowing that if the feds nabbed them and got a conviction, they would never see the light of day again.

When Roscoe and Damon saw the agents rush through the front door, they immediately reached for their loaded weapons. Before either of them had got off a single shot, both men had been sprayed with bullets. Damon had gotten shot once in the head and twice in the chest. He died with his gun still clutched in his hand. Roscoe was a little more fortunate than his dead partner. He was only shot three times; twice in the left arm and once in the leg, but he was still alive. Damon's body was taken straight to the morgue. Roscoe's was taken straight to the hospital, handcuffed to a gurney.

Two days later, the agents found out that the seized weapons from Roscoe's apartment were the ones that were used in their recent homicides. Roscoe was charged with the distribution of drugs, possession of counterfeit money, and the murders of Malinda Smith, Daniel DJ Twist Cooper, and his girlfriend, Kimberly Thomas. After Roscoe was released from the University of Pennsylvania Hospital, he was immediately taken down to the Federal Detention Center of Philadelphia.

One month later,
Wednesday afternoon

Waiting inside the FDC Philadelphia visiting room, Roscoe couldn't believe his worried, bloodshot eyes. Tori sat dressed up looking like a fashion model from out of *Vibe* magazine wearing Baby Phat, Apple Bottoms, and Gucci. He looked at his beautiful ex-fiancée and smiled. The expression on Tori's face was dead serious. She sat down directly across from him and looked into his confused eyes. Even when he smiled, all she saw was one of Satan's workers.

When Roscoe reached out his hand, she didn't accept it. Tori just sat there staring at him, letting the tears fall down her beautiful face. She could tell Roscoe had been stressing badly. He had lost some hair and much of his weight. The once big bad wolf was now looking like a skinny, lost crackhead. Like so many others before him, the feds had broken him also.

"Why did you kill her?" she cried out. "Why, Roscoe, why?"

Roscoe didn't say a word. He just looked at Tori and sadly shook his head.

"She didn't deserve to die like that! How could you be so evil? You're nothing but a monster, Roscoe! I'm happy that I never married you! God saved me from you. He knew that you were no good for me! I hate you, Roscoe! I hate you with every fiber in my body! I hope your evil ass rots in a prison cell. And when you die, I hope you rot in hell!" Tori stood up and said.

Roscoe still didn't say a word.

"I have one more thing to tell you before I leave."

"What's that?" Roscoe spoke up for the first time.

"That I did find me the man that I'ma spend the rest of my life with, and before you go, he would like to meet you," Tori said turning around and walking away.

Roscoe watched as Tori walked through the crowded visiting room and straight out the door. When he got back into his lonely cell, he walked over to the window. He had a good view of the outside street from where his cell was located. He watched as a red Range Rover pulled up and double-parked right outside of his window. Then he saw Tori walking across the street toward the truck. When she got to the truck, she stopped and turned around. She saw Roscoe's face looking out at her from the window.

The door to the Range Rover opened, and a tall, dark, and handsome, well-dressed man stepped out. It was Ricky. He and Tori hugged each other and passionately kissed.

The tears fell down Roscoe's gaunt face. The pain inside his heart was so much worse. After Tori walked around to the passenger door and got inside the truck, Ricky looked up at Roscoe and shook his head in total disgust. Then he got back into the Range Rover and sped off down the street.

Roscoe sat down on the edge of his cot and cried like the weak, broken man that he was.

"Thanks, India," Tori said, looking at India in the backseat.

"Anything for a friend!" India said with a smile.

After driving Tori over to her new apartment, India got in the front seat and said, "You'll be at the cub tonight, right?"

"I wouldn't miss it for the world!" Tori said smiling. "'Mr. Orgasm's' final performance. I can't wait!" She winked before walking inside her apartment.

Women were crowded on both floors and the VIP section. They were all cheering, whistling, and clapping while Ricky was doing his thing onstage. Money, bras, and panties filled the stage. Ricky had the club on fire! When his powerful exotic performance finally ended, he stood at the front of the stage looking through the large, boisterous crowd. He walked over and picked up the one yellow rose that was lying on the stage. His muscular, dark, sexy body was dripping with sweat. When the music stopped playing, Ricky raised his hand and asked for everybody's attention. Just like that, the entire club fell totally silent. Now all eyes and ears were on him.

"Ladies, as y'all know, tonight is my very last performance as a male exotic dancer." There were some cries, a few smiles, and hundreds of disappointed looks. "Every time, I gave y'all 110 percent! I would like to thank all of my fans that have been supporting me since day one. Thank you all so much for everything! This last yellow rose in my hand is for my soul mate, fiancée, and future wife. She is the woman who rescued me from myself!" Ricky looked through the crowd and saw all the familiar faces: Carmen, Tori, Keri and Teri, Sophia, Gloria, Victoria, and so many others.

When he jumped off the large stage, the crowd opened up like Moses opened the Red Sea. Ricky walked through the crowd of crying, smiling, and disappointed women with a smile on his face. When he finally made it to the opposite end of the club, India was standing there tearfully waiting for him. Ricky passed India the yellow rose, and the two of them began passionately kissing. Suddenly, the large crowd of women started cheering and clapping. All of India's prayers had finally been answered. Not only did she have the man of her dreams, she had finally gotten her yellow rose.

The Beginning . . .
because there is no end to true love!

Epilogue

"Mr. Orgasm"

Five months after being arrested, Roscoe was found guilty on all charges and sentenced to Federal Death Penalty. He'd finally gotten what he deserved. There was no greater satisfaction than watching justice being served. His ex-fiancée Tori began dating a doctor at the hospital where she works. She had been able to move on, despite all of the drama that was in her past. She was grateful for the chance to live the life that she deserved.

Gloria Jones finally divorced her wealthy husband, Larry. She got half of everything he owned. Now Gloria spends her days shopping and sexual nights with her tall, dark, and handsome new lover, Thunder.

Big Nook is now the manager of Club Chances. He retired from the police force to run the day-to-day operations for his two new bosses, India and Ricky.

Neo is now the number one exotic dancer at the club.

Victoria is still a teacher at the Community College of Philadelphia. She and Tom are still happily married, but once a week, they invite a young black stud into their bedroom to spice things up.

Nicole passed her psychology class with an A-plus grade.

Carmen and Hardrock got married and decided to move out to California. Now, every single night, Carmen shows her new husband all the sexual tricks she learned from being with “Mr. Orgasm.” Hardrock released his second album for Def Records. It sold 325,000 copies the first week out. And it later went on to sell over 4 million copies worldwide.

For his cooperation, Flex was only sentenced to nine-and-a-half years at a minimum state correctional facility in upstate Pennsylvania.

Nancy Robinson was arrested, charged, and convicted for the conspiracy to kill her husband. She was sentenced to life in prison. Now she spends all her time at the Women’s State Correctional facility, located in Muncy, Pennsylvania.

Ricky, India, and Asia all moved into a beautiful new home right outside of Philadelphia. They are currently preparing everything for their upcoming wedding and the birth of their first son.

Message to the Readers

The Curse of Unconditional Love. Do You Have It?

We've all been there a time or two. Falling head over heels in love with the person that we think is standing before us. One thing about the term *unconditional love* is that you'd practically do anything for that person. It's normal to have unconditional love for your parents and children. We expect that the love you have for them would never dwindle. Under that assumption, there is nothing that they could do to make you feel any differently. As a mother, I can look at my son and say that my love for him will always be the same. I can also look at my parents and feel the exact same way. However, outside of my siblings, there aren't really many people that I feel love this deep for.

Some people, not just women, have a hard time figuring out the difference. I could love someone or even go as far as being in love with someone, but is it unconditional? No, it isn't. Some people look at unconditional love as something great, but there are some situations where this could be totally the opposite. Some would say that this is ideal. This is the type of love you should strive for in your life. This is often spoken without actually thinking about what that means. To say that I love you *unconditionally* would mean that I love the good in you, as well as the bad. This means that I love you entirely. Instead of finding someone that loves the good, we expect that people should accept the bad.

So many people are cursed, and they don't know it. Women who actually believe that they are running away from you, when, in fact, God is distancing you far away from her. The curse that she possesses will continue to bring you down with her. They are the women who have been rejected by God. The people who run from relationship to relationship.

There are people who see no wrong in what they do and seek no correction. Then there are people who can't grasp any type of real happiness or comfort. The people who search their entire life looking for love through sexual gratification. They only find pain and heartache. The goal shouldn't be to receive unconditional love. I want to be told when I'm bad just as much as when I'm good. I want someone to help me be better instead of accepting all of the things I've done wrong.

The concept of unconditional love is dangerous because it can make people do some crazy things. It's one that should open your eyes to the world. Be very careful whom you love completely.

I believe that all love is conditional, especially in relationships. When it comes to feelings, we can all be hurt. We can all be broken and pushed to the point of no return. You can be hurt so badly that you make dangerous decisions. Many of these decisions could completely change the course of your life.

When love is good, it is amazing, but all too often, we give too much of ourselves to people who don't truly deserve it. This is in no way preaching to the choir. Most people who think they are in love can't even explain why they believe it. It's very easy to get so caught up on the idea of love that we totally miss all of the signs. Trust me, there are *always* signs; we just choose to ignore them because we are in love with the idea of being in love.

It may take a lifetime to find your soul mate and your one true love, but when you find it, you'll know why the people that you thought you loved . . . were merely an infatuation.

Live, Laugh, Love, and find your beginning . . .